LAMBS

Childhood Lost
Book 1

COLIN HARDIMAN

Writers South Press

CHARLOTTE, NORTH CAROLINA

Colin Hardiman/Writers South Press
Charlotte, North Carolina
Writerssouthpress@gmail.com
www.writerssouthpress.com

Publisher's Note: This is a work of fiction. Names, characters, and incidents are a product of the author's imagination. Locales and public names are sometimes used for atmospheric purposes. Any resemblance to actual people, living or dead, is completely coincidental.

All Scripture quotations are from the King James Version.

Cover photo by Patrik Stedrak/stock.adobe.com

Book Layout ©2017 BookDesignTemplates.com

LAMBS *Childhood Lost*/Colin Hardiman. -- 1st ed.
ISBN 978-0-9989985-0-3 [paperback]
LCCN: 2017907481

To Christopher, whose love, encouragement, and extraordinary wit saw me through this thirty-one-year project. He has been my greatest blessing, and may blessed Elohim always "make His face shine upon" him.

To Dad, who found salvation and forgiveness later in life, and finally became my daddy. His passing left only silence, as if part of the world died along with him.

And to my meek, lovely mother, whose life was filled with hardship and disappointment. Though she never seemed to care much for me, I tried to love her just the same. May she one day inherit the earth.

Fathers,
Provoke not your children to anger,
Lest they be discouraged.
Colossians 3:21

Contents

Ditches and Devils 1

When Rednecks Dance 19

Where Babies Come From 37

Unwanted Leftover 61

Running Away 79

Homes Sweet Homes 95

Any Port in a Drunken Storm 129

A Lazy, Crazy Interlude 147

The Codes 197

CHAPTER 1

Ditches and Devils

When I was growing up, living in rural North Carolina meant that all mailboxes were posted on the same side of the road. That meant some had to cross a road or busy highway to collect their mail. To add to this dangerous situation, there were folks (like my Great-Aunt Sophie) who had indoor plumbing, but did not have a septic tank. They either could not afford to install one; their land refused to perk; or like with my great-aunt, our local county officials hadn't gotten around to enforcing stricter sewer regulations on the older homes in the area. And *that* meant indoor sewage drained through underground pipes to a backyard cesspool or into ditches that ran along the sides of the roadway.

These two items (of little historical value) held an intimate meaning for a few unfortunates (like my Great-Aunt Sophie), because when they retrieved their mail from the box they could be standing over last night's supper or *"shit"* as Daddy called it. In the summertime, heat stirred the streams of black murky water, producing a most unwelcoming fragrance. Some left their mail in the box until after sundown, while others held their breath as they made a frantic dash to the mailbox and back. Then others (like my Great-Aunt Sophie) seemed to have either lost their sense of smell or had become accustomed to the off-putting odor, and ventured to their mailbox as soon as the mailman made his delivery. *But,* if anyone ever dropped a letter into one of those ditches, there it would remain until the chain gang arrived.

Every so often, convicts would clean out Great-Aunt Sophie's ditch by shoveling its contents into the back of a dump truck and (according to Daddy) disposed of it into *"Shit Creek"* just half a mile down the road from us. They were grown men—zebras on parade—moving ever-so-slowly in the heavy steel chains used to bind their legs. Each man was linked to the one beside him— a solitary thread that held together the empty faces of lost souls who were being punished for their crimes. The metal from those chains scraped the top of our road's dirt and gravel surface with every step they took. The sound it made was like a mournful tune, filled with remorse for some who had done wrong, while others echoed only regret for having been caught in the first place.

Sometimes their prison bus and dump truck drove up while my older brother Dylan and I were outside playing. Our mama, Irene, rushed us inside the house, telling us to *"hush"* and not to look out from behind the curtains at them, else they might see us watching, and that might make them mad.

"*Bad men,*" she called them, because they were paying for their sins.

While Mama hurried about the house, bolting the doors and cranking in the windowpanes, she reminded me of a wild animal desperately trying to save her young ones and herself from being devoured by a hungry beast. Even though prison guards stood watch over them—holding loaded shotguns—she was afraid some convict might get the notion to come to our house for an uninvited visit. My own childlike curiosity, though, made me peek around the curtains to watch those haunting men as they shoveled their lives away (that is when Mama wasn't looking).

Now, Daddy referred to this waste disposal system as "*shit holes.*"

"Stay away from the shit holes," he warned us. "The boogeyman lives in them ditches, waiting to snatch naughty little boys and girls down there to live with him."

Knowing a *shit hole* existed directly underneath your mailbox posed worrisome enough problems for adults when it came time to get their mail, but the thought of something related to *Old Scratch* living down there was frightening enough to keep a small child away—well . . . *almost.*

***

It happened during the spring of 1964, because I can recall a slight chill remained in the air. When I was growing up, we experienced four seasons in the Piedmont-Triad region of North Carolina. One rolled into the next without a hiccup. You knew where you stood with nature and dressed accordingly. And no one wore *all* white after Labor Day or before Memorial Day. Not even the poor.

After being confined to the inside of our house for the winter months, I longed to go outside and ride my tricycle, only I wasn't supposed to that morning. Mama had clothed me in the previous year's spring fashion, my light blue frock: the one with the bib collar trimmed in white lace and the sash in the back that formed a huge draping bow. Just to be allowed to wear this dress I would endure the stiff netting from the nylon crinoline petticoat that scratched against my bare legs and caused the dress's skirt to flare out. While I had nearly outgrown the close-fitting garment, it was still my favorite. In my only pair of black patent leather shoes and lacy white anklets, I was ready to go to town.

"If you go outside, Carrie Jane, you had better not get yourself dirty," Mama warned me. "Pansy will be here in a short bit to take us to do some shopping, and I will not have any nasty little children going off with me."

Pansy (*nee* Smith) was Daddy's mother; Dylan and I called her *Grammy*. She always took us shopping, because Mama's car would not run. My parents could not afford to get it repaired. In fact, they couldn't afford much at all, so Grammy paid for everything Dylan and I owned. She bought our clothing, toys, Dylan's red *Radio Flyer* wagon, my little red tricycle, and sometimes our food. I once overheard Mama say if Grammy had not made a few of our mortgage payments, we would have been homeless. I figured that was because Daddy did not work some of the time, after being fired or walking off a construction site for what he referred to as *"creative differences."* Mama called it being *"drunk on the job,"* only she was careful to *never* say such a thing around Daddy.

Of all the things Grammy ever bought for me, my favorite was the rubber dolly she gave me on my fourth birthday. It was a solid piece of dingy brown rubber from head-to-toe, molded into the shape of a little girl wearing a dingy brown dress. She wasn't pretty, but rather plain. Giving her a name did not seem important, because all that mattered was she belonged to me and me to her.

Mama didn't seem happy with my new friend, because she frowned and furrowed her brow when Grammy handed her to me. That night, she verbalized the reason for her displeasure to Daddy.

"Billy Ray?" (Mama called Daddy by his nickname, though his given name was William Raymond.) "You need to take a look at what your mother gave Carrie Jane for her birthday. I don't think she needs to be playing with such a thing."

"What the hell was my momma thinkin' . . . that looks just like a little a colored girl. Shit, I reckon we might as well let Carrie Jane keep it, because the gawddamn thing looks just like her," he chuckled. "You remember when they handed me Carrie Jane? Right after she'd been delivered? I laughed and asked that damn nurse: '*What the hell is that thing—some little colored baby nobody wanted?*' "

Mama didn't laugh.

Mama never knew what to make of my brown complexion and often referred to me as looking like "*Pansy's bunch,*" meaning some of Grammy's relatives, who were said to be Cherokee Indians. But she only said that behind closed doors, as if it was some disturbing family secret we had to keep hidden. Even Daddy's younger brother, John Sullivan (named after the last heavyweight champion to fight bare-knuckled boxing, who became the first heavyweight champion of gloved boxing), he often called me "*Little Pansy,*" saying how much I looked like Grammy when I was a baby.

Mama turned her head away from such remarks, but especially those made by complete strangers when we went into town. Perhaps if I had stayed close to Grammy, no one would have known that I belonged to Mama. No one would have asked why my hair, eyes and skin were brown, and my mother's skin so fair. No one would have questioned my mother with a hint of hesitation, "Is that one . . . *yours?*" Then Mama would not have stammered, her tongue tangled into a licorice twist, unable to proudly respond: "*Yes, of course she is my child; my own flesh and blood.*"

But it was only because Daddy *said so* that I got to keep my dolly. Though Mama *often* voiced her opinion on how things should be handled, Daddy always had the final say (especially when it came to punishment). Some nights my dolly and I hid inside the door-*less* closet of my bedroom—sometimes into the early morning hours—waiting for him to come home. Those were the nights he had been out drinking. Those were the nights Daddy got *really* upset after Mama told him Dylan and I had misbehaved. She called us *"bad children."*

"They need to be punished," she insisted.

Curled up into a corner of my closet, on the damp plank floorboards that separated my bottom from the earthen ground below us, my dolly and I waited for Daddy to bellow out my name. She would be the only friend I would have to share my fears with. I pretended she hugged me and told me how much she loved me (things my parents never did).

"Maybe I'll be okay. Maybe Daddy won't hurt me like he did before?"

My tears bounced off of her rubber body as I held her close, waiting to receive my sentence as one shackled, bound by a solitary thread of fate shared with my brother Dylan, who hid down the hall inside his own door-*less* bedroom closet.

When Daddy yelled out, *"Dylan . . . Carrie Jane . . . get your sorry asses into this living room right this gawddamn minute,"* I knew we would not escape punishment.

Before dolly, I remained hidden within the false security of my closet walls, pretending Daddy would never find me. Angry at my disregard for his authority, he charged into my bedroom in an explosive drunken rage.

"If you think you can hide from me, ya little shit, you gotta another gawddamn thing comin'!" he shouted.

Jerking me off of the closet floor by whichever one of my arms he could grab onto first, Daddy whipped me with his thick, black-leather belt as I dangled awkwardly in the air, and then tossed me onto my bed. Other times, he dragged me into the living room to join Dylan. Sometimes, he would hold one of us at a time above his head—with both of his arms extended—pounding our small bodies into the low-hanging ceiling to *"shake some gawddamn sense"* into us, while cleansing our souls with an asbestos shower as the overhead tiles crumbled.

When my dolly came to live with me, I feared Daddy might do the same things to her that he did to me. Instead of waiting inside the closet, I went before Daddy when he called out my name, but first I hid her beneath my bedclothes, so he could never find her. She would be one of the few things during my childhood that Daddy did not take away from me.

But, it was on that particular spring morning in 1964 that I picked up my dolly, and together we went outside by our front door and sat upon the concrete slab (supported by unstable cinder blocks) that we used for a front stoop. They belonged to the same family of cinder blocks that supported our house. The blocks used to keep our shell-of-a-house off of the ground had proven more durable than the rotting boards of the house's exterior. Its interior revealed walls that had never been painted, door frames without doors, floorboards that were never covered, and plumbing that seldom worked in the three-year-old incomplete structure.

The mailman came that morning with his usual 9:30 delivery. My dolly and I waved to a greying, bushy-haired man, who sat hunched over the wheel of a faded green jeep.

"Hey, Mr. Sweeney!" I shouted from across the road to him. "My dolly says, '*Hey*,' too!"

Mr. Sweeney leaned out of the jeep's opened side window and pushing his hand upward, returned our wave.

"Why, good morning to ya, Carrie Jane and your dolly. My, aren't you two dressed up real pretty this morning?" His wooly mustache wiggled as he smiled at us.

I smiled back.

"My mama says we're going to town."

"Well, I hope your dolly and you have a most pleasant trip," he said.

"Thank you, Mr. Sweeney."

Wishing us a "*good day*," our mailman continued on with his route.

"See, even he knows you're real," I told her just as Mama and Dylan came out of the house to go across the road to our mailbox—staked in the ground right next to Great-Aunt Sophie's.

"Are you still talking to that stupid doll?" Dylan asked me.

"She's not stupid. You're stupid!" I briefly stuck my tongue out at him.

"Carrie Jane, stop acting ugly towards your brother, or else I tell your daddy, and he tans your little behind," Mama warned me.

"Yes, ma'am."

I knew better than to say or do anything bad to my brother, but sometimes I couldn't help myself—especially after Dylan started it.

As they walked away, it occurred to me that I wanted to go with them.

"Mama, Mama, Mama," I shouted, pushing myself off of the stoop. "Can me and my dolly come, too? Can we?"

"No, you're too small, Carrie Jane. You wait right there until we get back," Mama stated in her stern *do-as-you-are-told-or-else* voice.

She took Dylan's hand as he skipped along beside of her, leading him towards the mailboxes. He glanced over his shoulder at me. His well-coiffured Princeton shimmered golden-brown in the early morning sun. His pale skin reflected light as if made of porcelain. Dylan was a pretty boy . . . a doll with blue eyes. Mama often said so. (Except for her shoulder-length dark, wavy hair and lovely green eyes, he looked just like her, but then everyone said that Mama looked like a young version of the actress Ava Gardner.) When she wasn't looking, Dylan contorted his *puggish* nose. A snake-like tongue slithered out from between his teeth for my benefit. When his face returned to normal, he smiled. His facial expressions made me angry. Dylan could be an ugly child.

During our childhood, Dylan's sole purpose in life seemed to be in trying to make me angry. He never wanted a sister, because sisters were no fun to play with. Daddy agreed. He wanted only sons. Daddy blamed me for having been born a girl, a fault in my development he said I should have corrected before being delivered.

Now, perhaps my sex had displeased my father and brother, and the color of my skin annoyed my mother, but as a child I would not be ignored. Nor would I be left out. Perhaps I was too short to reach the mailbox, but so was Dylan. Mama always lifted him up, so he could take the mail out of the box. Dylan was exactly a year, a month, a week, and a day older than me, and if he got to go to the mailbox, *well*, so would I.

Clutching my rubber dolly, I nestled us onto the seat of my tricycle. Then holding her on my lap with one hand, and the other firmly grasped around the handle's right rubber grip, I decided to ride us to the mailbox. The previous warnings I had received from Daddy *not* to ride my tricycle into the roadway didn't mean much to me at that moment, because I pedaled as fast as my small black patent leathers would move the foot pedals. Looking down, I watched the front wheel bump over the scattered gravel that covered the road's dirt surface, never once checking my left or my right before crossing, to make certain no vehicles were traveling towards me. With all of the energy I could muster, I forced the three-wheeler to the other side of the road to the ditch's edge, just underneath our rusted mailbox. It was there we got off the tricycle, and I gave Mama my best, *"See what I just did—ain't you proud of me for being such a big girl"* smile.

Instead of receiving praise, Mama's voice ripped through me, letting me know I would be punished for my mistake.

"Carrie Jane, what do you think you're doing here? You could have been run over! I *told you* to stay at the house, you hardheaded child. Just wait until your daddy gets home!"

I looked down at my feet until tears blurred them from sight. Then I shook as one overcome with a great fear—a fear that only the small, the innocent, the ones who have suffered at the hands of unmerciful giants know.

Perhaps what happened next was from the sudden fear of Daddy's belt. Or perhaps I was just a clumsy child and slipped on the gravel. Or then perhaps the boogeyman stuck a hand out of the *shit hole* and grabbed me by the legs. Whatever caused it, my dolly and I suddenly plunged (*headfirst*) into the ditch.

Total darkness surrounded us as we were taken down in the pit and sucked into the black regions of the monster's belly. The sound of rushing water roared in my ears while my arms flapped about wildly, like the wings of a bird trapped inside a steel cage. My mouth opened to breathe, only it sucked in the fluid that had already filled my nostrils. The more I panicked the more waste went down my throat. It tasted of spoiled prunes that had been soaking in warm beer. And I knew what beer tasted like; Daddy often fed sips to Dylan and me of the foul-tasting liquid.

Struggling inside that darkness, I believed Daddy's warning: It *was* the boogeyman that had taken hold of me. It felt as if he was pulling me down deeper and deeper into his hole. All of the times Daddy told me that if I was not a good girl the boogeyman would get me had finally come true. I had not minded Mama, so he snatched me into the ditch to live with him, *forever.*

Then suddenly, I felt Mama's hands clasp around my ankles, and she tugged and yanked with such force that old devil finally let go, and I was pulled free of the ditch's hold. Standing me onto my feet, Mama slapped me across the back as I wheezed and hacked, spitting up a dark, clumpy substance. Liquid streamed from my nose and mouth. Unable to see, I wiped at my eyes with my muck-covered hands. At that moment, I realized something was terribly wrong.

My empty hands reached out, searching for something that was no longer there. My dolly had not come out with me. The boogeyman had kept her as his prize. My need to save her threw me once more to the edge of my nightmare, only this time Mama grabbed me by the collar of my dress before I could take my half-blind, second leap.

"Carrie Jane, what is the matter with you? Sometimes you just don't have good sense!" Her words echoed in my ears like the distant sound of a mother crow scolding its young.

"*Ma . . . ma . . . doll . . . eee!*"

They were the only words I could choke out to tell Mama that my friend was drowning, and we had to save her. Mama ignored my asthmatic plea, as she half-led, half-pushed me back towards our house.

"I guess we won't be go shopping now, and it's your entire fault," Mama said as she removed my dress and petticoat and tossed them into the trash.

"No," I coughed.

"If you think for one moment, young lady, that I'm putting those nasty clothes into my washing machine, you've got another thing coming. Besides, they're getting too small, and your Grammy will be buying you another spring outfit before too long."

"*No!*" I spat out.

"Shut up," she warned me, "or else you'll be feeling the palm of my hand against your face."

I chose weeping.

As Mama sat me down into the bathtub and began washing away my misadventure, Dylan appeared inside the bathroom doorway holding a bottle of nose spray. The five-year-old's chin quivered into a cluster of dimples. The blue of his eyes melted. Eyes once made of ice pooled, then spilled over the rims.

"Does my sissy need this?" he whimpered.

Though it was the only time during our childhood he would ever show me any compassion or come to my aid, this simple act of kindness obliged me to become his champion for the next ten years.

***

That night, Daddy bellowed out my name after Mama told him what I had done. If I remained hidden within the three walls of my closet, he would find me, so I crawled out on hands and knees. My legs trembled as I pulled myself up by the side of the bed. I flipped back the bedclothes to see if, perhaps, my dolly had returned to me. She hadn't, and Daddy was growing impatient.

"*When I tell you to do something I mean now, gawddamnit—not tomorrow!*" he roared.

I heard one of his steel-toed work boots stomp the living room floor. Edging myself along a bedroom wall to the doorway and slipping silently into the hall, I then tiptoed my way into the living room. A light from the overhead fixture glared down upon me. I saw the back of Daddy's head as he sat in his brown vinyl swivel rocker. Still. Unmoving. Daddy must have sensed my presence, suddenly swinging himself around in his chair to look at me. His eyes were smoldering black coals. The red streaks that surrounded them bloodshot with fiery anger. I shivered as one overcome with a great fever, chilled to the bone. Tears rolled over my eyelids, bouncing off the high cheekbones supporting my pudgy, round face.

"I ain't hit you, yet, so stop your damn blubbering. Now, sit your sorry ass down on the couch!" Daddy ordered.

He had never told me to sit down on the couch before. The few words he used while disciplining me were usually drowned out by my screams as his belt pounded upon my flesh. I slid my hands underneath my thighs—body tensed—awaiting his next move.

Daddy turned away, leaning back in his rocker, with a cigarette in one hand and a beer bottle cradled in the other. He took a sip from the bottle before setting it on top of the unlit Monogram kerosene-burning stove standing next to him.

Then Daddy began to chuckle. The chuckle deepened into a coarse laugh as he ran his free hand over the top of his pompadour hairstyle.

"I'll be damned," he laughed, "I've heard of a shit eatin' dog, but this is the first gawddamn time I ever heard of a shit eatin' young'un!"

As he reached for the beer, his laughter stopped. He then spun himself around in his chair to face me. His eyes were not his own—eyes I had not seen before, yet, felt. They belonged to my devil in the ditch—eyes full of fire and brimstone. He leaned into my direction—breath hot with smoke—preparing to devour me. I tried to scream, but nothing came out. Not a sound.

"*By gawd, Carrie Jane, you're one more damn, dumb young'un,*" he hollered. "*If you ever pull another stupid-ass stunt like that again, I'll take that gawddamn tricycle of yours and back over it with my truck a couple of fuckin' times. Let's see if you can ride that piece of shit ever again. And then I'll tear yer scrawny butt apart, 'til you won't be able to sit that ass of yers down to take a piss, let alone a shit. I'll even throw you back into the shit hole where you belong. Understand me, gawddamnit?*"

Then the boogeyman disappeared.

Daddy once more leaned back in his vinyl rocker and held the cold beer to his head, while gently swaying back and forth with his eyes closed, as if his brain pounded from pain.

"Get your ass to bed," he muttered.

Daddy did not beat me with his belt or slam me into the ceiling that night, because it would be one of those rare occasions he found humor in my bad behavior. But, I believed every word my daddy *ever* said to me. He was the terror of my young life, even more so than the boogeyman in the ditch.

A few weeks later, I stood upon a chair in the living room and stared through the window panes, watching the chain gang as they shoveled out Great-Aunt Sophie's ditch. As Mama closed the curtains before me, I somehow knew my life would never be to the same.

Some different, more permanent tears now blurred my eyes. I was, in fact, alone.

Then, as Mama predicted, Grammy bought me that new spring dress, only this one was yellow with a huge draping bow, but without the crinoline petticoat. Fashion and times were changing. In a few short years, I would be too big to ride the tricycle, yet, tall enough to reach the mailbox. The chain gangs would no longer come to visit us, as sewage lines and septic tanks would replace ditches and cesspools. Our mailbox would even be moved from across the road to the end of our driveway, so Mr. Sweeney had to deliver the mail along both sides of the roadway. Our dirt road would *eventually* be paved in asphalt, with a bright double-yellow line painted down its center. Progress would change many things for the better, though my troubling, lost childhood would remain frozen in time for many years to come. Even Dylan's moment of compassion for me would soon fade from our world of ditches and devils into one of nothingness. Nothing real worth remembering; nothing real worth treasuring, except for the one thing that really mattered to me while growing up . . . a simple, nameless, rubber dolly.

CHAPTER 2

When Rednecks Dance

I t was the dead of winter, January 1965. The ground was frozen solid without moisture, and the lifeless trees, with their naked branches, hovered gloomily over small children. Black limbs cast a shadow against a threatening grey sky that seemed to whisper, "*Snow.*" But after several hours of running back and forth to look out the living room window, and then asking Mama every five minutes when the snow was coming, that optimistic energy Dylan and I had created would be shattered. The snow would not come to us that Saturday; only a shower of sleet and frozen rain. Like with most things during that period of our childhood, we had to wait (even on the new baby Mama kept promising us.)

"Mama, when's our new baby comin'?"

"Oh, it will be here in a few weeks," she would reassure Dylan and me.

Having just turned five years old, I still had no comprehension of time.

"But Mama, how long is a few weeks? Is it a real long, long time? And what if the baby don't come then? Does the stork take it to somebody else's brother and sister?"

"Listen here, young lady, the baby will come when it's supposed to come and not any sooner, so stop asking me any more of those dumb questions!"

It did not take much for me to upset Mama, especially at times like those when she looked down on me as if I was a peculiar smelling creature: her green eyes opened wide, nostrils flared, while holding her breath to not breathe in the air surrounding me, as if my ignorance might be contagious. I kept my mouth closed for the time being, before she took a notion to slap me across the face or take a hickory switch to my backside or worse . . . *tell Daddy.*

"Carrie Jane, you're a dummy," Dylan said, looking to Mama for approval.

"Sometimes she can be," Mama agreed.

I stuck my tongue out at Dylan; sometimes I didn't like him.

***

Like most Saturday mornings, Daddy left us to spend the day at his father's garage to have a *"few beers"* with their *"drinkin' buddies,"* as Daddy referred to them. One particular fellow showed up there every Saturday. He was this lanky, haggard looking, stoop-shouldered alcoholic, with greasy salt-and-pepper seasoned hair. He went by the name Earl Putnam. His weathered appearance made him look sixty, instead of his actual age of forty. After World War II, he introduced himself at William Raymond Murphy Brine's garage and never went away. Over the years, Raymond (as most folks called him), acquired such a fondness for him that he often referred to Earl as his *oldest son.*" Even Daddy shared a strong brother-like admiration for the man, especially when it came to Earl's notorious reputation as a brawler and his ability to pummel another human being to a pulp with his *mean* right.

"Yep, that ole Earl's so strong, he could have easily whupped the *Brown Bomber*, Joe Louis, with just one hand," Daddy boasted. "Why, Earl once beat a man and left him for dead on the side of the road, simply because the son-ov-a-bitch wouldn't dim his headlights.

"And ole Earl's always gettin' his self arrested for beatin' the tar outta people, and it seems like he winds up before this same Guilford County judge . . . *Branson, Brannon,* or was his name Brown? Naw, that's the name of the son-ov-a-bitch who arrested him. Hell, if I can remember. Anyway, he's stood before this judge over at the courthouse every single gawddamn time. So, one day, that judge finally had enough and ordered Earl to never strike another man with a closed fist and condemned his hands as lethal weapons. If he had to fight, the judge told him to use an opened hand or else spend the rest of his life in jail.

"Not too long after that, we was over at the VFW having ourselves a few beers—*and minding our own gawddamn business*—when some asshole starts this bar fight, pulls out a Hawkbill knife, and slices Earl's left arm *wide* open, all because Earl was slappin' the crap outta him . . . just like that judge ordered him to do. So, later that night, he borrows my daddy's pistol and goes after that son-ov-a-bitch.

"Now, I ain't saying Earl had anything to do with it," Daddy smirked as he told us, "but the very next day they found that same piece-ov-shit tossed into a ditch along the side of some dirt road over yonder in Randolph County. He'd been shot through the head. The county sheriff tried to arrest Earl for it, but he never could prove he'd done it."

Both Grammy and Mama failed to understand the reasoning behind Raymond and Daddy's admiration for such a person. While Grammy seldom spoke ill, judgmental words about anyone (well, except for her late step-father Silas Simpson and grandmother Mary Catherine, *and* her brother-in-law Chester), one day she broke her silence on Earl to say she just plain couldn't stand that *"no 'count, white trash."* Even Mama swore him to be the *"meanest, vilest man"* she had ever laid eyes on, who would one day get Daddy into all manner of trouble if he continued to associate with him. They were careful to *never* say such things around Raymond or Daddy.

Since their Saturday drinking sessions lasted all day and usually way into the night, we rarely saw Daddy until Sunday morning, sometimes passed out on our living room floor or on the couch, *that is,* unless Mama told him that Dylan and I had misbehaved, and Daddy first gave us a beating before heading off to bed. His normal routine, though, would be altered on this particular Saturday.

Just as a dark grey haze overshadowed the evening sky, and the sound of sleet tapped against the windowpanes, our telephone rang. As Mama answered, we could hear Grammy's voice screaming through its receiver as if she was speaking through a public-address system, causing Mama to hold the upper portion of the receiver away from her ear.

"Irene, Billy Ray is bleeding! He is bleeding all over the garage, and it looks like he is going to bleed to death!"

"Pansy, what are you talking about?" Mama's face turned ashen. She always called Grammy by her given name.

"I tell you what, Irene," she continued shouting, *"Billy Ray is going to die if he doesn't get some help real soon! Some of his fingers look like they are barely hanging on, and he won't go to the hospital. He says there isn't anything wrong with him, but he is so drunk he doesn't even know what is happening."*

Through her hysteria, Grammy managed to explain how Daddy had decided to play mechanic on his white 1961 Ford F-100 truck. As he was attempting to unlatch the pickup's hood, Earl grabbed Daddy around the waist and tried pulling him away; only his fingers were still clutching the truck's metal grill. Daddy was so drunk and cold he never felt the grill's edges slice into his fingers like dull razors, cutting one to the bone. It was only after his blood began to trickle down the truck's grill and front bumper, and from Raymond shouting at them, that Earl let go of him. Daddy bled for several long minutes before Raymond (whom Grammy claimed was a little less intoxicated than the others) became worried and told her to telephone Mama.

She sent word through Grammy to tell Daddy that he needed to go to the hospital emergency room over in High Point to have his hands looked at *"right away!"* He relayed a simple three-word message back to her: *"Go to Hell!"* It was not until Daddy was about to collapse from too many beers and blood loss that he finally agreed to let Grammy drive him home.

Dylan and I watched from the living room window as Grammy's green 1959 Plymouth Suburban station wagon pulled into our yard (the one I had disabled a week before after pushing in all of the buttons to its PowerFlite transmission panel, just to see how it worked.) Not only were Grammy and Daddy inside, but Raymond and Earl, and some other drunk we knew only as Larry. While Grammy remained warm inside the idling station wagon, the four men emerged, staggering forwards then backwards like unbalanced giants. When Mama opened the front door for them to enter, a mixture of alcohol and slippery ice took hold of their bodies, and the giants fell over our threshold, turning the living room into a threshing floor.

Dylan and I ran for cover behind Daddy's brown vinyl swivel rocker, where I placed my right thumb inside my mouth, because it made me feel invisible. So, when I poked my head out from behind the rocker to watch the giants, I pretended they could not see me.

Daddy lay at the bottom of their heap, with his hands wrapped inside bloody rags. As one kicked at the man on top of him, another attempted to use the man underneath him to support his weight, as he pushed himself upright. Each man struggled to get onto his feet, but as soon as one was able to stand and attempted to help another off of the floor, he would be pulled back down into the pile of giants. It turned into a drunken redneck hoedown, performed to the patter of cursing, angry gents.

"Get the fuck off me, ya son-ov-a-bitch!"

"Ouch, asshole!"

"Move yer gawddamn foot 'fore I shove it up your ass!"

"Ouch, dumb shit!"

Then Raymond (whom Dylan and I called *Paw*), being a little soberer than the rest, choreographed a routine of his own. After rising to his feet, he braced the backside of his six-foot four-inch frame against a living room wall for support, then leaned over at the waist to help one of the men stand. During his first rehearsal, Paw lost his balance and fell back among the group, but on his second attempt he took hold of Earl's scarred, calloused hands and jerked him with such force, Earl was off the floor and in Paw's arms.

As the two men embraced, I giggled: "Dylan, you think they're gonna dance?"

"*Shut up!*" He hissed.

"*You shut up!*" I hissed back.

Dylan thumped me in the back with a fist. He could see me. Dylan could always see me. I wanted to hit him in return, but knew he would only strike me a second time and harder. I ignored him.

A moment later Paw changed partners, pulling Larry (a pudgy, red-faced, straw-haired giant) to his feet. Then the three men lifted Daddy off of the floor. As Mama led them into the kitchen, I turned to Dylan.

"You wanna go watch?" I asked him, taking the thumb from my mouth.

"No," he replied.

"I'm goin'."

"You do, and I'll tell Mama," he promised me.

I stuck my tongue out at him. Jumping up, I returned the thumb to my mouth and once more became invisible. Following a trail of blood drops into the narrow kitchen, I inched my way through a forest of human legs and noise, until I found the pair that belonged to Daddy. Someone had propped his tall, muscular frame against the kitchen sink, so he could rinse his hands under the water faucet.

"Get this gawddamn thing the hell outta my way!"

Daddy's speech was slurred and forced as he attempted to knock a dish drainer off the kitchen counter. Mama barely caught the falling dishes and drainer in her arms before moving them to the stove's surface.

On tiptoes, I edged my nose over the counter top, so I could peer into the sink. At first, all I could see was Daddy's face. His was a handsome, if not, pretty face. Though he looked like a young Paw, with his fine chiseled features, Daddy's dark eyes and hair denoted that something more than just Irish blood ran through his veins. Even Daddy often said, when trying to explain the difference between his red-haired brother and himself: *"Johnny might have the money, but I've got the looks."* His complexion, though, seemed to be fading to pale as I watched him lean further into the sink.

Something else caught hold of my attention—something so frightening I could not look away. As the water flowed over his fingers, blood intermingled with flesh, and both flowed rapidly down the drain. Meat that looked like uncooked strips of bloody chicken with gristle and bone lay open before me, while a fingertip appeared barely attached by a piece of skin. My trance was broken when Daddy slipped and fell to the floor, and my thumb came out of my mouth.

"Irene, get that child out of here!" Paw screamed at Mama.

She led me into the living room where Dylan joined us on the couch. The room smelled of alcohol, stale cigarette smoke, and garage grease. I became even more frightened by all of those towering giants being inside our small house. They were not of human form, but more like the monsters that appeared in my nightmares. In my dreams, they stomped through my bedroom, so enormous that their blocked heads made of steel seemed to tear through the ceiling. If I remained still within my bed, they might pass by without doing me any harm, but if I moved they would yank me from my bed with their massive hands, crushing me between them. It seemed my only protection was by placing my thumb inside my mouth, so the imaginary giants of my dream world could not see me at all. But those four monster giants inside our home were real—more real than the ones in my dreams—and I feared they would hurt Mama, Dylan, and me, and even our new baby should it come while they were there. Even my thumb could not protect us. I clutched one of Mama's swollen sides.

"Raymond!"

"*What?*" Paw stomped into the living room, as if agitated by the sound of a woman's voice speaking his name.

"Raymond, you had better get Billy Ray to the hospital." Mama spoke with the timidity of one afraid to address giants. She always called Paw by his given name.

"I ain't goin' no gawddamn where 'cept back to the *gay*-rage," Daddy said as he rounded the corner from the kitchen into the living room, with his eyelids half closed. He staggered into Paw, who took him by the shoulders to steady him. Blood was soaking up the material of the kitchen towels someone had wrapped around his hands.

"Get him to the hospital, now! I mean it, Raymond, before he bleeds to death," she spoke up.

"I ain't goin' no gawddamn where," Daddy repeated himself, sounding more disoriented with every word.

"Come on, Irene, now you just let the man alone and stop your naggin'. Billy Ray'll be fine once he sleeps this off."

As Earl spoke those words, Mama's head jerked in his direction. She glared at him, with her eyes bulging and teeth clinched. At first, I thought she might tell Earl what she said about him when Daddy and Paw were not around, but she turned her attention back to Paw, ignoring his presence.

"You either get him out of here and take him to the hospital right this minute, or I will . . . I'll call the sheriff!"

"No, you won't," Paw scoffed at Mama, while Earl and Larry laughed in her direction.

"Oh, I *won't*, will I?" Gaining control over the giants, she pushed herself up from the couch and waddled towards the telephone.

"I'll kick yer fuckin' ass if ya do!"

Daddy's legs buckled underneath him as he attempted to swing one in her direction. The two other drunks rushed in to support his weight.

Mama paused for a moment as if having second thoughts, but then she picked up the telephone's receiver and dialed zero.

"Watch me," she promised.

A woman's voice echoed from the receiver. *"Operator . . . this is the operator . . . who are you trying to call?"*

"I need the county sheriff's office," Mama said, placing the receiver to her ear.

"Okay, okay, calm down Irene, we're leaving; we're leaving right now, just don't you go calling the sheriff on us. Let's go, Billy Ray; we're taking you to the hospital," Paw said, pushing Daddy towards the front door, but Daddy pulled away.

"I ain't goin' to no gawd-damn *horse*-spital!"

"Yes, you are . . . Earl, Larry, grab him," ordered Paw.

Paw took the lead, wrapping his arms around Daddy's chest from behind, while the two other men clung onto Daddy's biceps. As he struggled to free himself, the foursome spun about the room, completing the final waltz of the drunken rednecks. Then stumbling out the opened front door, they slipped off of the icy stoop and fell onto the frozen ground into a heap of pickled flesh. As they floundered about, like fish out of water, Paw was once more the first one off of the ground. Though Daddy tried to push him away with his useless hands, Paw shoved him into the backseat of Grammy's awaiting car. Daddy could be heard cursing the night air, until the three men locked him inside, and Grammy drove them away into the darkness. And Mama hung up the telephone.

"Mama, if Daddy goes to the hospital, will he die? Daddy says only old people go there to die," I said, afraid I would never see him again.

Her body trembled, as tears formed in her eyes.

"No . . . no, he'll be fine. The two of you need to go on to bed, so I can clean this mess up," Mama replied, her voice trailing off.

The next morning, I jumped out of bed and ran into my parent's bedroom to find Daddy lying there next to Mama. His hands were wrapped in gauze bandages, stained with dried blood, and he was breathing. He awoke and stared at me as if irritated by my presence.

"What in the hell is your gawddamn problem?"

"Nothing," I whispered, as embarrassed tears swelled up in my eyes.

"Then who in the hell gave you permission to come in here?"

"Nobody."

I looked down at my feet and scuffed them awkwardly on the floor, only to look up and see Daddy had raised a hand to strike me. I flinched, but he pulled back as if he thought better of it.

Though their bedroom did not have a door, we were often warned to never enter without permission. It was a punishable offense.

Then Dylan came running into the room, like an excited little boy on Christmas Day.

"Daddy, Daddy, can I see? Can I see your hands, please?"

"Yeah, why the hell not?"

Daddy sat up in bed, unwinding the bandages. The gauze stuck in places where dried blood had adhered, causing him to wince and groan with each tug. He stretched forth his fingers for us to view, in an admiring sort of way. They were black and blue and red, more than twice their normal size. Threads were sewn in all directions, as if an inexperienced seamstress used a sewing machine to stitch together damaged fabric.

"You know what? Some colored man sewed me up. I wasn't gonna let him touch them, but the hospital said he was the only doctor they had working. Can you believe it—a gawddamn colored doctor? *Jee—sus!*"

Daddy held his hands close to his eyes for a better view. He smiled to himself, as if in awe of his mangled fingers. This was his prize for being a man who could drink himself into the abyss, face *Death* square in the face, yet, live to tell about it.

"Yep, that colored doctor told me if it hadn't been so damn cold, I'd most likely bled to death," Daddy bragged.

✳✳✳

When the time came for Daddy to have his stitches removed, he decided to take Mama, Dylan, and me with him. The hospital said he needed to see the original doctor who had treated him.

His name was Dr. James Johnson, and he was working out of his practice on Washington Street that day. It sat right in the heart of High Point in an area both the whites and blacks referred to as *Colored Town*. Specialty stores, professional businesses, and houses lined both sides of the street, owned and patronized by the local black population. As children, Daddy told us that no white person in his or her right mind would go there alone, because black people would do all types of terrible things to them. Even when drunk, he would never explain what those *terrible things* were when I asked.

"Roll up the windows and lock the gawddamn doors," Daddy told Mama as he got out of the truck at Dr. Johnson's office. "You never know what-in-hell might happen to you around here."

He took the truck's ignition key with him.

Dylan and I sat quietly, exchanging frightened, wide-eyed glances whenever we saw a black person. I was so afraid I had forgotten to put my thumb inside my mouth to become invisible.

Then an old black man came walking towards our truck. He smiled a near toothless grin in our direction, waved, and shouted to us.

"Hello, there! How y'all doing?"

Perhaps what I did next was a result of being told by my parents to be polite to my elders, of whom I did not realize excluded elderly black men. Perhaps it was just an involuntary reflex when someone waves at you. Or perhaps it was just plain stupidity on my part for not thinking about what my parents would do to me, because the next thing I knew my right arm and hand were returning the old man's greeting. It was then I felt the sting of Mama's hand upon my legs.

"*Don't you wave at those colored people,*" she hissed at me.

"Carrie Jane, you're a real dummy." Dylan always had a way of reducing me to what he thought was my simplest form, while in search of Mama's approval.

"Sometimes, I think you don't have the good sense God gave you, because you sure don't know how to use it," Mama chastised.

Dylan smiled.

On Daddy's return, the first thing Mama did was tell him what I had done. As he reared his right arm into a striking pose, I cowered down into the bench seat between Mama and Dylan, awaiting his blow. But, something about his hand distracted him, and he pulled back as if he thought better of it. He called me an ugly name, but then added the word "*lover*" to it.

I did not understand.

We were well away from Washington Street before Daddy started trying to wiggle his scarred fingers.

"Humph," he snorted and sniggered to himself. "That colored man seemed to know what he was doing."

***

Within less than two weeks of Daddy's accident, Dylan and I finally received our long-anticipated snow. And even the new baby came a few weeks later, just like Mama said. As for Daddy, he continued going to Paw's garage nearly every Saturday to get drunk. So did Earl. No one but Mama and Grammy seemed concerned he had nearly removed Daddy's fingers from his hands.

"Pansy, I'm starting to believe that Earl cut Billy Ray's fingers open on purpose, because he's jealous he's not Raymond's son," I overheard Mama tell Grammy.

"I've been thinking the same thing, Irene," Grammy agreed.

But they were careful to *never* say such things around Paw or Daddy.

CHAPTER 3

Where Babies
Come From

W hen the time came for our new baby to be
delivered, Daddy and Paw were working at
a construction site in Chapel Hill. Earl had
joined them. They claimed the less than hour-and-a-
half commute was too far between here-and-there, so
the threesome spent the weeknights at some cheap
motel in Chapel Hill. Mama had been on the telephone
all that evening trying to reach Daddy to let him know
the baby was on its way, only there was no answer in
his motel room. She began pacing the living room floor
like an anxious cow, embracing the mound of flesh she
had grown in her abdomen.

"Oh, Billy Ray," she groaned, "I hope you haven't
gotten yourself into another mess."

A few weeks had passed since Earl nearly cut off
Daddy's fingers. While they were almost healed, Mama
became even more fearful that Earl's shenanigans

37

would send Daddy to jail . . . *or worse.* It seemed that Earl didn't just destroy men's lives; he took their souls, as well. Sometimes, I overheard Mama on the telephone with Grammy, discussing how Earl ran his own local version of what they called a *Redneck Mafia*: selling guns, stolen merchandise, pornographic films, and non-tax-paid liquor. Or how he and his twin brothers-in-law, Roy and Ray Reynolds, hung out at truck stops along I-85, selling amphetamines to long-distance truckers. Mama only knew of such things, because Daddy told her.

Sometimes, late at night (while pretending to be asleep in my bed), I even overheard Daddy tell Mama how Earl had *"tricked"* him into committing crimes.

"Ole Earl first told me that some man hired him to unload the back of this tractor trailer, and he'd pay me twenty bucks to help him out. But when we'd nearly finished the job that stupid son-ov-a-bitch decided to tell me every gawddamn thing inside was stolen."

"I hope you left once you found that out!" Mama's voice elevated, sounding as if shocked that such behavior existed in men.

"Hell no I didn't leave! I promised Earl I'd do the job, so I finished and got paid my twenty bucks. But I told him I wouldn't be doing any more of that shit!"

Or the time Daddy told Mama how Earl asked to meet him outside Smithy's Saloon, a tavern inside the city limits of High Point.

"Ole Earl, he says to me: '*Billy Ray, pull your pick-up truck around back and keep the engine runnin' while I take care of something inside here.*'

"The next damn thing I knowed, here comes Earl hightailing it around the side of the building like his gawddamn pants are on fire. He jumps in on the passenger side and slams the door shut. About that time, I see this policeman reach in through the opened window and grab Earl by the right arm.

"'*You're under arrest!*' he yells at Earl.

"Then ole Earl—that scrawny-ass son-ov-a-bitch is strong as a gawddamn ox—he yanks that policeman's hands loose like he's plucking ripe tomatoes off the vine and takes *him* by the gawddamn wrists.

"'*Drive!*' he hollers at me.

"So, I floor the gas pedal, draggin' that man alongside the truck. When I get up some speed, Earl lets go of him. I'm lookin' in the rear-view mirror, and I see that lawman flip-flop every-which-a-way on that gravel parking lot," Daddy chuckled.

Mama didn't laugh.

"*Billy Ray . . . how could you?*"

"Don't '*Billy Ray*' me. It ain't my fault you came from a bunch of gawddamn Puritans!"

I did not understand.

I had always been told police officers were our friends and only bad men hurt them. There were many things during those early years I did not understand.

But, in that present moment, Mama desperately needed to find Daddy. I fell asleep in my bed that night to the clicking sound of the telephone's rotary dial, as she continued her search for Daddy.

***

It was around midnight when I was awakened from the warm stillness of my bed by my mother's pain-filled voice.

"You need to get out of bed, Carrie Jane. We are going to the hospital," she groaned.

I did not understand.

"Mama, why we going to the hospital?" I yawned and tried to wipe the crusty sleep remains from my eyes.

"We are going to get the new baby there."

"But Mama, I thought the stork was going to bring the baby."

"There's been a change in . . . here, put your robe on over your pajamas and slip into your bedroom shoes," she ordered me through clinched teeth.

"Mama, why cain't I put on my clothes? It's cold outside. Will I freeze? Will our new baby freeze, too?" I had never been any place outside our house in my pajamas before.

"There's not enough time to get dressed."

A strain I had never heard before crept into Mama's voice. Her chest heaved as she gulped in large portions of air. She sat down heavily onto the edge of my bed.

"You sick, Mama? Is that why we going to the hospital? But Mama, only old people go there to die. That's what Daddy says."

"*I'm fine*, Carrie Jane. Just don't ask me any more questions," Mama warned.

Dylan stood in the doorway to my bedroom dressed in his pajamas and robe, all droopy eyed, with sleep still swimming about his head. I looked to him for a response, but he would not say anything.

"Come on, Pansy just drove up. We need to go," she told us.

The February night air seemed bitter cold, biting at the exposed areas of my face and hands. The cold even penetrated the terry cloth material of my bathrobe, given to me by Daddy's brother (whom Dylan and I called Uncle Johnny) and his wife, Aunt Roberta, as a Christmas present. Even Dylan received one. Mine was pale blue, and just below the left front shoulder, Aunt Roberta embroidered my initials *CJ* in navy-blue thread. Dylan's bore an emerald green shade, with a large white *D* embroidered on his. Whenever we wore our new robes, it usually turned into a fight.

"My robe is nicer than yours, Carrie Jane, because my *D* is bigger than your *C* and *J*," he taunted me.

"Huh-uh, ain't done it," I countered. "Mine is nicer, 'cause I got two letters and you only got one!"

Dylan usually punched me in the back to let me know I was wrong, showing me that he did not like my attitude. But on this particular night, we were both a bit too tired to fuss with one another.

Grammy told us to cover up with a blanket she had placed in the back of her green Plymouth station wagon and for us to take a nap. But as she drove us away into the darkness of the unlit country roads, I tried to understand what she was saying to Mama.

"I don't know why they have babies delivered at hospitals these days. We did fine back when I had my children. Why I bore Billy Ray and Johnny in the front bedroom of Raymond's sister's house across the road from you, only it belonged to his parents Luther and Sarah Jane at the time. I never had a doctor—just my mother-in-law Sarah Jane and sister-in-law Sophie—and I never had a problem. Now they say you need to see this so-called *baby doctor*. I s'wanee, they're just trying to find ways to take more of your money these days," Grammy snorted. "Driving to High Point in the middle of the night to have a baby . . . just don't know what this world is coming to."

Mama never replied. She managed a low moan from time-to-time.

***

High Point Memorial Hospital was an obscure, burnt-orange shaded facility, with yellow brick accents during the daylight hours. Part of the hospital appeared to be five stories in height when it suddenly dropped to three stories, and then the next section rose to four, then down to one level, like children's building blocks stacked in no particular pattern. Come nightfall, the structure changed in appearance, as streetlights illuminated a foreboding, shadowy image against the moonlit sky.

Grammy steered her car towards the emergency room, which also served as a garage to house ambulances and other hospital vehicles.

"*Humph!*" She grumbled, after being unable to find a place to park. She piloted us to the front entrance, where we all got out. Faceless people in white outfits emerged from within and put Mama into a wheelchair to take her away.

"Where you taking my mama?" I screamed, chasing after them down the sidewalk and into the hospital's lobby.

Every bit of Grammy's five-foot, three-hundred-pound framework proved too quick for me, as she grabbed onto the back collar of my robe.

"Carrie Jane, don't you worry about anything. Your momma will be just fine," Grammy said, as the people in white pushed Mama around a corner and out of view. "And I want Dylan and you to wait right here in this lobby, while I go park the car and then find a telephone to call your daddy. And make sure you mind yourselves."

Dylan and I stood together in silence. White-painted cinder block walls faced us on both sides. Portraits of greying, unsmiling men dressed in business suits hung upon them. Their condemning eyes stared down at us as if they were saying we did not belong there; only the old, sick, and dying entered their sacred doors. A strong odor of rubbing alcohol clung to the air. Polished light grey tiles—glistening with the brilliance of veined marble—covered the floor. I leaned over to catch my reflection in one of them.

"Why, what are you two little children doing here this time of night?"

I looked up to see an old man in a wheelchair being pushed in our direction by a woman dressed in white.

"We're waiting on our grandmother," Dylan replied to the old man.

"Well, if you two aren't the cutest little things I have seen in a long time. Come over here, and let me give you both something," he said, his voice rattling, as if it had worn out from years of use.

Dylan walked closer, but I stayed at a distance, suspicious of what this old man was going to do to us. He reached inside one of his white robe pockets—as white as the coarse strands of hair remaining on his head—and took out two foil-wrapped pieces of chewing gum. He handed one to Dylan.

"Now, you come over here little girl, so I can give you a stick of gum, too," he said to me.

I inched forward, snatched the gum from his shaking, wrinkled hand and then jumped behind Dylan.

Mama (and even Grammy) told us to never talk to strangers or get too close to them, because they might grab us and take us away, and we would never be seen again. And we never-ever accepted candy from strangers, because it might be poisoned. As far as I was concerned this old man was a stranger, and I was not about to chew his gum. When the old man was out of sight, I turned to Dylan.

"Hey, Dylan, you want my gum?" I asked.

"Sure," he said and stuffed it into one of the pockets on his robe.

It amazed me, how after all of the warnings Mama and Grammy had given us about taking candy from strangers, that he was not worried about chewing poisoned gum.

"*If he dies,*" I thought to myself, "*it'll be his own fault.*"

"Well, I could not find your daddy," Grammy huffed, as if out of breath from having run a marathon. "I'll just try to call again . . ."

"*Grammy?*" I interrupted her, frantically yanking at the skirt of the snug-fitting green dress she wore.

"What is the *matter* with you, Carrie Jane?"

"*Grammy . . . Dylan . . . this . . . this . . .*" I found my own self—huffing and puffing—unable to get the words out.

"Calm down, child!"

Before I could tell her how some old man had given us chewing gum—*which was probably poisoned*—and how Dylan had kept his, who should roll by us again, but that same old man.

"Are you children still here? Why let me see, I think I have some more gum in my pocket. Here you go." He handed us each another piece. "My goodness, you two are most certainly the prettiest little children I've ever laid these old eyes upon."

"Dylan, Carrie Jane, now I want you to thank this kind gentleman," Grammy ordered us.

I peered up at this strange woman standing in front of me—an oversized bush supported by two legs. This could not be *my* grandmother; she would never allow us to take poisoned chewing gum from a complete stranger!

"Thank you," Dylan replied.

"Carrie Jane, now where are your manners?" she insisted.

"Thank you," I muttered.

Then the woman in white rolled him away for the second time. Dylan gladly accepted my second piece of gum when I offered it to him.

"Dylan, Carrie Jane, it looks like you two will be staying with me until your mother gets out of the hospital. I guess we'd better go," she said.

I did not understand.

None of this made any sense to me: hospitals, babies, and storks, taking candy from strangers. I had a lot of questions to ask somebody.

We were almost out the front door when another woman dressed in white—wearing a funny-shaped white cap that didn't quite cover her head—came running after us.

"*Wait!*" She shouted. "*You can't leave just yet!*"

Then Mama appeared, being wheeled towards us. She did not look well, slumped slightly forward in the wheelchair. Mama was having difficulty sitting up, as her watermelon-like stomach now laid low in her lap.

"*Pansy*," Mama gasped, "I won't stay in this hospital. We have to get to Asheboro right away. They won't allow my doctor here, and the only doctor they have working tonight is a colored man."

Mama's face reddened as she trembled from a spasm. "I told them that no colored man was going to deliver my baby."

"What do you mean her doctor can't deliver her baby here?" Grammy spun her round body on the people in white, like a fat cat preparing to attack its prey.

"Mrs. Brine's obstetrician, Dr. Hall, is not allowed to practice medicine at this hospital. His privileges have recently been suspended. He can only deliver babies in Asheboro's hospital. If she wants to have her baby here, our Dr. Johnson is on duty and he will deliver it for her." A robust woman in white, who spoke with the huskiness of a man, stood rigid against Grammy's challenge.

"Yes, and he's colored. No colored man is going to deliver my grandchild," Grammy snapped back. The smiling dark eyes of my fifty-year-old grandmother hardened, taking on the appearance of a warrior readying for battle.

"If you do not like what our hospital has to offer, you can go elsewhere, but I suggest you do it soon. Mrs. Brine's contractions are not far apart, and her baby might deliver sooner than you would like." The woman in white crossed her oversized arms in defense of her territory.

Grammy paused for moment, as if debating on whether to fight or take flight. As she ran her fingers over her teased, dyed reddish-brown hair, she let out a snort.

"Humph! You can count on us going elsewhere! Dylan, Carrie Jane . . . you two wait right here with your momma, while I bring the car around," Grammy instructed us.

"*Why would a colored doctor-man deliver our new baby?*" I silently asked myself. "*Storks were supposed to do that!*"

Nothing made sense.

"But Mama, what happened to the stork? We not getting our baby, now?" I asked her.

Mama lifted her bowed head. Her disheveled dark brown hair appeared moist from sweat. The area around her eyes looked dark, like black rings circling two green globes. Her lovely white-satin skin had turned grey. My pretty mother did not look like herself. The only makeup she ever wore was red lipstick on her full lips. Even when my mother worked as a runway model at the largest department store in High Point, she only wore red lipstick on her face. People said Mama did not need to wear makeup; she had a natural beauty. Mama liked being a model; only Daddy said he did not want her to model. Mama said that was why we were having a baby.

She placed a hand to her dry, cracking lips as if she was going to be sick. She belched, then placed her hands onto her abdomen and looked at me.

"Carrie Jane, would you just be quiet!"

Dylan snickered at me. "Mama told you."

I stuck my tongue out at him and was about to call him an ugly name when I heard an old, familiar voice.

"Why there you are? I believe I have a couple more sticks of gum in my pocket for the two of you." The old man was back. "Here you go."

He handed us another piece of gum, smiling at us like an old grandfather. His tired blue eyes appeared cloudy and almost grey under the stark hospital lights.

Something about the old man frightened me. Was he trying to be nice, or did he just want to make sure he did the job right when he killed us? Was he there to die, or was he already dead? I had never seen a dead person before. And did he ever sleep, or did he just ride around the hospital in his wheelchair, day and night, looking for little children to poison with his endless supply of gum? I kept remembering what Mama had said so many times before: *Don't talk to strangers! Don't take candy from strangers!*

"What do you say to the nice man?"

It was the voice of my mother, expecting us to thank a complete stranger for candy. Perhaps I was still asleep in my own bed dreaming and none of this was happening.

Dylan said, "Thank you very much," but I uttered a half-hearted, *"Thank you."*

The old man patted us both on the shoulder.

"Mind your parents," he told us and was rolled away by the woman in white.

"Mama, Mama, Mama, is this gum poisoned? You told us to never take candy from strangers, and Dylan kept his, and what if we die, we'll never get to see our new baby, and . . ."

"Carrie Jane, would you stop asking me any more of your stupid questions and shut up!"

Mama did not need to tell me again.

Grammy returned for us and helped Mama inside the car. This time the people in white only stood and watched. Hurt and confused, I remained quiet on the long ride through the city and into the countryside towards Asheboro. I sat in the backseat with the last piece of gum clutched tightly in my hand, trying to understand what was happening.

"Carrie Jane, do you want that piece of gum?" Dylan asked.

I handed it over to him without a word. It suddenly occurred to me that he had a pocketful of sweet gum, and I did not have any. And I liked chewing gum—especially the fruity-tasting kind the old man had given us. I would wait until he started chewing it to see if he lived. If he did, I would ask for mine back.

The next thing I remembered was Grammy telling me to wake up, because we had arrived at Randolph Hospital in Asheboro. The people in white once more took Mama away, and Grammy told us to stand in a hallway while she tried to find a telephone to call Daddy.

I leaned against an off-white cinder block wall of the sterile-smelling facility. One side of my face pressed onto its cold surface. I shivered. The hospital's glaring lights reflected off the tiled floor into a flash of exaggerated brightness—starbursts and sprays of yellow, orange and white light. I closed my eyes. I heard the people in white as they spoke in low, hushed tones. Their words faded into the abyss of my mind. Words were falling, falling all around me. Then silence.

"Why, little girl, what are you doing here this time of night?"

I opened my eyes.

From around a corner a woman dressed in white appeared, running behind the old man in his wheelchair, pushing him towards me. A cloud of black smoke and sparks burst forth from the tires, leaving a trail of fire behind them. An evil roar tore loose from his mouth; only this time it was not the old man's voice I heard.

"Wee--ll, Miss Priss, I'll tell you why: It's because you never left! Now, I won't ever let you leave, because you've been a bad girl, asking too many of your stupid questions. But then you are always a bad girl. Just ask your momma, and she'll tell you. And you want to know something else, the new baby she keeps promising had sure as hell better be a boy! If it's another damn girl and comes out lookin' like you that gawddamn colored doctor can keep it for himself. But as for you, Carrie Jane, you need to come on

over 'ere and chew a piece of this poisoned gum. Did you hear me, young'un? Right this gawddamn minute, you little shit!"

"You thank the nice man for his poisoned gum, Carrie Jane, or I'll tell your daddy when he gets home that you were a bad girl and didn't mind your mother. Then you'll get a spanking."

I turned to this voice and saw Mama. She was sitting in a wheelchair next to the old man, with Dylan standing beside of her, smiling and handing me all of the gum from out of his robe pocket. I could not move, my feet frozen to the floor from fear.

"I said for you to get your sorry ass over here before I stomp it!" the old man shouted.

"I finally got ahold of Billy Ray, and he's on his way back. Lord have mercy, Carrie Jane . . . you had best wake up, child! Don't you be standing out here in this hallway and go to sleep. I s'wanee, you're fixin' to fall and hurt yourself doing something silly like that. Let's go home, so I can put the two of you to bed."

Grammy's voice came closer to my ears, and the old man and Mama disappeared. The next thing I remembered was waking up on Grammy's den couch, with Daddy leaning over me.

"Wee--ll, Miss Priss, I hope you're damn-well happy, 'cause you got a little sister." Daddy slurred out his words, exhaling the remnants of a fermented beverage into my face. "Yep, you got a gawddamn little sister. Naw, I couldn't have another boy, but another

gawddamn girl. What in the hell ya got to say for that, huh?"

There was nothing to say worth suffering a blow from Daddy's hand. I kept my excitement over a new baby sister to myself.

"Good-gawd, another gawddamn girl," he complained until later that evening when he returned to Chapel Hill. "Hell, now I've got a damn good excuse to go get drunk!"

***

The next day, Grammy decided she wanted to visit Mama and the new baby (whom my parents named *Dinah*) at Randolph Hospital. I did not want to go back there. Though it was a different hospital, I feared that old man might be waiting for me, but Grammy said I had no choice in the matter; I was too little to stay by myself. To make things worse, the people in white would not allow Dylan or me to see Mama, because hospital policy required children to be twelve years and older before they could see patients. As if that wasn't bad enough, Grammy brought along her older sister, Great-Aunt Ruby, to watch us in the hospital waiting room while she visited.

Both Daddy and Paw said they hated Ruby, only Paw never said why. Daddy preferred to put his hatred into words, especially after he'd been drinking.

"That sorry gawddamn woman is nothing but an evil, lying, thieving bitch! One day my daddy went to put some money away in his sock drawer where he always kept it—'cause he ain't trusted banks since The Great Depression—and he finds there's $4,000 missing. He asks Momma if she took it.

"'Naw,' she tells him, 'Henry Myers from just down the road came up here the other day and went rummaging through your things. He must've taken it.'

"So, Daddy says, 'I'm gonna go kick his sorry ass, and get my money back!'

"Momma's like, 'Naw, naw, just let it go, Raymond. Let him keep the money.'

"But Daddy says, 'I'll be gawddamned! I worked too hard for that money.'

"As Daddy's heading out the door she hollers: 'I took it! I took your money, Raymond! Ruby made me do it. She said if I didn't give her $4,000, she'd put a curse on Carrie Jane, and I couldn't let that happen.'

"Daddy then asked me to go with him over to Thomasville to this run-down mill house where Ruby lives, so I'd stop him from killin' that voodoo witch. Gawddamn if he didn't get mad, and he sure-as-hell lit into her.

"'If you ever step foot back onto my property, steal any more of my damn money, or threaten another one of my grandchildren with your voodoo bullshit, I'll put a curse on you by way of my size fourteen, steel-toed boots up your gawddamn ass! Now, give me my damn money!'

"That old toothless, gummy bitch grinned in his face and said: '*Why Raymond, I ain't got no i-dee what you're goin' on about.*'

"You could tell she was lying—standing there with those flabby-ass arms wrapped around that big ole *fat* belly of hers like she was trying to hide something. You could just tell. For a minute, I thought my daddy was going to stomp that fat ass of hers right there on the front porch, but he later said he didn't want to go to jail for beatin' that pure evil-ass woman.

"The next day, Daddy opened up a savings account; he said as much as he distrusted the damn banks, he'd rather take his chances with them over Ruby. That crooked-ass bitch never gave back the first gawddamn red cent of that money she stole. No one ever said what she did with it, but one thing's for gawddamn certain: It wasn't spent on new teeth!"

Despite what happened, Grammy kept in contact with her sister, but feared she would be found out.

"Now, Dylan and Carrie Jane, you children promise me that you won't tell your Paw, your daddy or your momma that your Aunt Ruby came with us to the hospital. And while I'm upstairs visiting with your momma and your new baby sister, you two behave and mind Ruby," Grammy said before leaving the three of us in the hospital's waiting room.

"We promise," Dylan and I echoed our responses.

Great-Aunt Ruby found herself a comfortable chair to relax her short, plump body and then lit a Lucky Strike cigarette. Straggly silver and black hairs stuck out around her head from her trying to pull what little thinning hair she had into a bun. Deep lines creased the sagging dark flesh of her face, creating sacks that hung from her high cheekbones. Since Ruby did not have any teeth (not even a set of dentures like Grammy), her thin lips had turned inward. When she took a drag from the unfiltered cigarette, her face rolled over her gums, deep inside her mouth, almost to the bottom of her nose and chin. She made me shiver, as if I was standing in the presence of something dreadful.

Afraid of what to say to her, I walked over to Dylan, who sat on the far end of the waiting room reading some children's books he had brought with him.

"Hey, Dylan, can I read one of your books?" I asked.

"No," he replied, never looking up while flipping through the pages of a Little Golden Book. "You can't read!"

Dylan did not share.

So, there I stood—a five year old with nothing to do but suck up Great-Aunt Ruby's smoke and watch Dylan read books. It was then I noticed a yellow toy dump truck, a box of crayons, and a doll lying on a table in the opposite corner of the room. I took a seat on a wooden child's chair next to the table. The dump truck did not interest me, and there wasn't a coloring book to go with the crayons.

Picking up the doll, I examined her for a moment. She was dressed in white, wearing the same funny-shaped white cap that didn't quite cover her head, just like the women working inside the hospital. Her complexion was almost as white as her clothing, making her faceless. I wondered what she would look like if even darker than my own brownish-toned skin.

Removing the doll's white dress and cap, I took the black crayon from its box. With long strokes, I began to color the doll's body. Then I started coloring in her face. The doll was beginning to take on a new life. Coloring the doll black did not make her any different from when she was white, I reasoned to myself. Just black. I could not understand why everyone made it sound like a bad thing to be a colored person, because everyone was colored—some just darker than others. When I finished with her I decided that I was going to color my own skin black to see if it made me different. Her face was almost complete when she was suddenly snatched from my hands.

"Little girl, we do not color our baby dolls to look like *Negroes*! If you want to color something, I will get you a coloring book." A faceless woman in white stood over me, clutching my new friend.

The sudden realization came to me that I had done something terribly wrong. It was one thing to color your own doll, but not one that belonged to the hospital. Then the fear of Daddy swept over me. If he found out what I had done, he would surely give me a beating I would not soon forget. And it would not be for just damaging the doll—but for coloring her *black*.

I turned to look at Dylan. He would tell on me, because he could not resist the opportunity of watching me get punished. As I glanced over at him to receive his

I'm telling on you smile, he seemed too absorbed in his books to take notice of anything else.

There was still Great-Aunt Ruby as a witness to my misdemeanor, seated just a few feet away. Since nearly everyone (especially Mama) made it a point to tell Daddy everything I had done (mostly wrong), there was no reason to believe she would be any different. As I held my breath, my eyes moved cautiously into her direction. A smile had parted her rubbery lips, while the lit cigarette drooped from a corner of her mouth. She let out a hoarse chuckle. The raucous noise rolled up her chest and out of her mouth, but she sucked back on the cigarette too soon and began to choke. It seemed like several moments passed, as Ruby gagged on spit and smoke, then entered into a coughing and wheezing fit. Regaining her composure, with the cigarette still clinging to the corner of her mouth, she took another puff.

"Ya know somethin'," Great-Aunt Ruby finally managed to speak—her deep, raspy voice sounding as if she gargled with bits of shaved metal, "your daddy used to do some mighty peculiar things when he was a lil'un, like once huggin' a hen's biddies until he took the very life outta 'em, 'cause he thought they needed a nap, but I done reckon you got him beat."

The woman in white returned with a coloring book, but without the doll. When Grammy came back, Ruby did not tell her what I had done, which made me think she wasn't a completely *bad* person like Daddy said. But at the age of five, I still had a lot to learn about just how wicked some relatives could be.

As for Daddy, he never found out what I had done to the doll, nor did he learn of how Grammy allowed Ruby to baby-sit us at the hospital. Then, again, the authorities never found out about his involvement in unloading stolen merchandise and dragging a policeman across a parking lot under Earl's command.

Our crimes and transgressions went unpunished.

CHAPTER 4

Unwanted Leftover

Our winter melted away, bringing in its place the scent of short-lived tree blossoms and the smell of freshly mowed wild onions. Even though the warm spring sun shined down upon us, I could still feel a slight chill left behind—a chill that would grow colder as the years passed. While Daddy's verbal and physical abuse left me a frightened, angry child, my inability to develop emotionally could not be blamed entirely on him. My mother failed to nurture me, leaving me with a hollow heart.

Daddy often boasted that when I came into the world, Mama performed only the basic duties of a caregiver: *"She gave you a bath, a bottle, changed your diaper, and then threw your ass right back into the crib. You were a good baby."*

But Mama's problem with me began before then. For some reason, I made several attempts at an early delivery, requiring her to take this medicine with a real long name and too many syllables to pronounce in one breath. She cried every time she visited her *baby doctor*, because she accepted his bleak mantra of: *"You will not carry this baby full term."*

Grammy, though, had faith in my ultimate and timely delivery.

"One day, after your momma came home from visiting with that *baby doctor* of hers, I decided she'd had enough of his hogwash, so I called him on the telephone.

"*'When is that baby due?'* I asked him.

"*'On such-and-such a date,'* he told me.

"*'Well, then that's when the baby will be born,'* I said.

"And then I politely asked him to hush up and stop upsetting my daughter-in-law, or else I'd be making a trip to his office," Grammy often told me.

Exactly nine months to the day, I was born. But every year on my birthday, instead of receiving a birthday cake, Mama reminded me of the burden I had been for her to bear: an *"almost miscarriage"* as she preferred to call me. I supposed that meant the diaper knot—tied around the stork's beak—nearly came undone during my delivery.

And then there was the other *teensy* problem: My mother never anticipated having a dark-eyed, black-haired, brown-skinned baby girl (the polar opposite of her blue-eyed, bald head, pale-skinned baby boy.) I suppose my hair color changing to dark brown at the age of five was some consolation.

When I was growing up, Mama never showered me with affection or words of praise. She never said, *"I love you,"* and never smiled at me. If I ever came close to her—like a stray cat that rubs up against a stranger for physical contact—she hugged her chest, never allowing a hand to break free and pat me on the head or shoulder, unless to push me out of her way.

I can recall two memorable acts of kindness Mama performed during my childhood: the time she pulled me from out of the *shit hole*, and when she had Paw rush us to the doctor's office after Dylan accidentally split my head open two weeks before Dinah's birth. (Dylan happened to be pounding a crossbar to our partially-constructed swing set into the cold, hard ground as we sang *I've Been Working on the Railroad*, when he swung the metal object over his head to gain momentum and planted it into the top of mine.)

For her motherly duties, Mama kept my clothes clean and prepared my meals, but her contempt for me surfaced after Dinah's birth, especially during the times I became ill. Oh, she'd give me that nasty-tasting, burgundy-colored medicine when I suffered from a case of worms, sometimes a dose of castor oil or cod liver oil, or that brown laxative (the maker swore was chocolaty tasting) when constipated. When I was four, she even took me to a doctor to find out those itchy, scaly patches on my eyelids and face was eczema. At first, she rubbed an ointment onto my afflicted areas, but soon realized it to be a waste of her time and left me to my scratching.

Then from the age of five onward, illness struck me late every fall season when I came down with a wrenching hack-up-a-lung, puke-out-your-guts case of the croup. Late at night, for two weeks or longer, I was awakened by this uncontrollable cough that forced me from my bed and onto my feet, so I would not choke on the thick green mucous purging from my sinuses and lungs. Pacing the floors, I walked continuous circles through the house starting from my bedroom, into the kitchen, then the dining room and living room, hallway, and back into my bedroom, stopping every few feet and retching out a cough. Sometimes, when I could finally catch my breath, I lay down on the floor and wept from the pain.

If Daddy happened to be home when one of my nightly coughing fits set in, he shouted at me from his bed to *"shut that shit up!"* It was when Daddy screamed, *"Don't make me get out of this gawddamn bed and come in there,"* that frightened me the most.

Feeling fear and shame for being sick, I cupped my hands over my mouth to suppress the coughing, only to find myself dry-heaving over the toilet bowl. Though my mother got out of their bed to feed the new baby, she seldom found the desire to help me.

"Go get some water to drink and then go back to bed," my mother yelled at me from under their covers.

Drinking water proved useless. Most of it I hacked onto the floor. Since my parents seldom took me to the doctor, and only purchased over-the-counter cough syrup or lozenges if someone else was sick, that left me with the task of trying to figure out how to stop those incessant coughing fits on my own. I began licking the salt from saltine crackers or eating table salt directly from the shaker, which seemed to help at first, but ultimately made it worse. Out of sheer desperation, I foolishly swallowed Vick's Vapor Rub, with my childish reasoning of: *"They make cough syrup, so this should work!"*

Sometimes during the cold season, when Mama and the others fell sick, she brewed up this homemade elixir of brown sugar and onion she kept warm for hours on top of the living room's kerosene heater. She would give me a single teaspoon of the mixture and then (to my confusion) throw the rest of it out.

Even the times I accidentally cut myself, jammed a piece of glass into my foot, or crushed a fingertip, I had to figure out how to stop the bleeding and bandage the wound on my own. And if something became infected, I had to devise ways on how to stop the pus from breeding out of control, with hot rags, table salt, and rubbing alcohol. Whenever Dylan became sick or injured himself—like the time he slipped into a tub of scalding water and burnt both hands—Mama doctored him through all of his ordeals. Perhaps my mother taught me a lesson in self-reliance at an early age, because as I grew older I no longer relied on her for anything, and sometimes felt I had *raised* myself.

***

The day Mama and Dinah came home from the hospital, Aunt Roberta joined us. The six of us rode home in Grammy's station wagon: Aunt Roberta in the front passenger seat next to Grammy, while Dylan and I sat in the backseat alongside Mama and the new baby. Mama had no more sat down when she lifted Dinah off of her lap and above her head to take an admiring look at her latest acquisition. Dinah's tiny white head—*the whitest head I had ever seen*—bounced against the station wagon's ceiling. A blood-curdling howl resonated from the *weest* mouth I had ever seen, along with Mama lamenting, "*Oh my baby, my poor little baby. Did I hit your soft spot?*" Cradling the newborn in her arms, she caressed Dinah's round, bald head until she calmed down.

Once we arrived home, Grammy and Aunt Roberta joined us inside and sat on the couch watching as Mama fed the new baby, until Dinah decided to spit-up some of her bottle-fed formula.

"Oh, goodness," Mama cooed, "I need to get a cloth to clean your little face."

I thought I was going to be the helpful big sister, rushed into the kitchen, found a dishtowel lying in the sink, and returned to wipe Dinah's mouth with it.

"How could you be so stupid as to use that nasty rag on my baby's face? Are you trying to kill her?" Mama screamed at me in front of everyone.

I should have realized that something was questionably strange about that towel, but I was a five year old in a hurry. While its outside had dried and felt crinkly to the touch, the inside had remained moist, feeling like a glob of cold, wet oatmeal in my hands. Then there was this offensive, sour odor—kind of like that forgotten pack of leftover bologna Mama once found inside the refrigerator—that should have triggered my immature senses. The bologna was covered with fuzzy patches of blue, green, and white.

"Ooh, that's so purty," I told her. "Can I have it?"

"For goodness sakes, *no* you can't have that boloney! It's rotten and will make you sick as a dog," Mama scolded me for asking such a thing.

Now, lacking good judgment with no company around was one thing, but a public display that embarrassed Mama (especially in front of Aunt Roberta) would not be forgiven or forgotten.

Aunt Roberta was a petite, *put together* woman of German stock, whose short-cropped greying hair, horn-rimmed glasses, matching outfits, and well-maintained home reflected order. Comparing Aunt Roberta to my mother was like comparing a Mercedes to a Corvette: the first a durable, precision-engineered model, able to withstand whatever road hazards life had to offer, while the other was a stunning two-seater, with sleek lines, and great handling, only its fragile outer shell cracked under pressure. So, when Aunt Roberta made a hasty retreat for the front door, I knew I was in serious trouble.

"Pansy, we need to be going. I have to tidy up the house and fix supper before Johnny gets home from work," Aunt Roberta announced in her matter-of-fact tone.

As they got into Grammy's car and drove away, all grew deafeningly silent inside our little house for a brief moment. The calm—*some say*—before the storm.

"How dare you embarrass me like that in front of Pansy and *Roberta* of all people? I'll bet she'll go off and blab to everybody that I keep a dirty house. Everybody thinks she's such a wonderful housekeeper. See how well Roberta would do if she had three children to look after. You mark my words: Miss *Run-Her-Mouth* Roberta will tell what happened here today. She'd enjoy making me look bad, thanks to you." Mama's voice grew more resentful with every word.

"You're nothing but a mean, hateful little girl, Carrie Jane. And if my baby gets trench mouth, it'll be your entire fault!"

Unable to control myself, I burst into tears.

"I'm sorry, Mama. I wanted to be big sissy and help. I won't do it again."

"No, you won't do that again, because I had better not ever catch you *touching* my new baby, you hear me? If I do, I'll smack you in the face so hard your head will spin!"

Mama rarely threatened punishment, unless she intended for Daddy to give us a beating, which meant Dylan and I suffered internal anxiety until he returned home. If she felt we needed to be punished immediately, and no hickory switch was available to whip our backsides, Mama improvised with the palm of her right hand smacking against our faces, causing the teeth to chatter and neck snap to one side. If not for Grammy and Aunt Roberta being in the room, I imagined she would have slapped me without warning.

Tears seemed to be my only solace for the moment, fearing that what I had done might harm my new baby sister. From Mama's point-of-view there was no excuse for my actions, not even the fact she left that soiled dishtowel in the sink before going to the hospital. And though Dinah never showed any signs of illness from my shameful mistake, Mama told Daddy once he returned home from Chapel Hill, who gave me one of his alcohol-induced tongue lashings.

"Only a damn dumb shit would pull such a stupid ass stunt! Hell, what I flush down the gawddamn toilet is smarter than you!"

Then he chuckled at his own words, meaning I would not receive a beating.

Being the middle child meant that I had become the loneliest, most overlooked person in the family. So, the first time I sought to be in the company of my mother and baby sister, Mama came up with a plan to keep me busy and out of their way. She lowered the ironing board, plugged in the iron, and told me to press pillowcases and handkerchiefs. Being an awkward five

year old, I burned myself—*a lot*—which meant I cried—
a lot!

"Stop acting like such a baby, and go put some butter
on it," Mama scolded me. "It's just a little burn. You
certainly know how to make a mountain out of a
molehill."

As for Dylan, he seemed to take the arrival of Dinah
in stride and ignored her, though it meant Mama could
no longer mollycoddle him as much with a new baby to
take care of. That didn't keep him from being spoiled.
Grammy (along with Daddy and Mama's approval)
made sure he received the more expensive toys to play
with, and he had more clothes in his closet to wear (his
closet being nearly three times the size of mine),
simply because he was a boy. Both Daddy and Mama
gave him the second largest bedroom in our house,
filled with a solid-oak bedroom suite Grammy
purchased from a high-end furniture store in High
Point.

The headboard to his bed contained bookshelves on
each side, as well as a center cabinet with a sliding
door. The matching oversized dresser, chest of drawers
and nightstand had antique brass swing pulls on every
drawer, and a wood-framed mirror mounted to the
dresser.

Of all the furniture Dylan owned, the pieces I envied
him most were the child's oaken roll-top desk and
swivel chair. Sometimes, when Dylan left his room
unattended, I would sneak in and sit down at his
treasure. The desk appeared boyishly masculine, yet,

elegant, with its tiny drawers and hidden compartments. After running my fingertips along the half-round slats of the tambour door—creating that *rat-a-tat* sound—I slid the lid up and down to hear the soft rippling noise it made as it moved inside the smooth tracks. I then pulled my legs and feet onto the armless chair's seat and spun around in circles upon it four-legged platform—raising it up, then down in the opposite direction—making myself dizzy drunk.

"Stay out of my room and leave my things alone!" Dylan shouted, as he rushed into his bedroom to punch me in the back for having dared touch his property.

Of course, I never listened.

My own bedroom was an unfinished laundry and sewing room, with a hot water heater taking up half of the closet space. A 1920s Singer Sewing Machine, with a seven-drawer wood cabinet and supported by a white cast-iron base, stood alone in a corner. Mama used it more as my changing table than a sewing machine. Sometimes (when Mama went outside to hang clothes on the line), I sat down upon the Singer's treadle and rocked it back and forth just to watch the band wheel spin.

I slept in a baby bed until the age of four, when one morning I stood up and the particleboard bottom gave way beneath me, and I went crashing to the floor. Fortunately, I suffered only a few cuts and bruises, but I needed somewhere else to sleep, and Mama swore it would not be in my parents' bed. So, Daddy found me a secondhand plywood, brown-stained, flat headboard and bed frame for ten dollars, and Grammy bought a cheap set of twin box springs and mattress to complete my bed. A few months later, she shopped the discount furniture stores around High Point for a dresser and chest of drawers (crafted out of questionable material), saying she simply could not afford to pay for two expensive bedrooms at the same time on her limited store charge account.

Both the dresser and chest of drawers looked as if someone covered them in cheap brown paint, leaving a lackluster finish that felt tacky to the touch. If you pressed your hand against their surfaces for less than a minute, the heat and sweat produced by your palm caused it to adhere to the finish, leaving behind a gooey hand print. Even the brown painted knobs stuck to your hands when opening a drawer. Using furniture polish made it even stickier.

I hated my furniture and hated feeling like a forgotten leftover in the refrigerator. So, one day I decided that ugly brown paint must go. Removing one of Daddy's welding rods he kept inside a rusted toolbox on my closet floor, I slipped between the dresser and a wall, and started gouging the welding rod into one end of the furniture's surface. The finish peeled off like thick paste, revealing particleboard underneath. Then I dug deeper, turning some of the areas to sawdust, while leaving a mess on my bedroom floor. I brushed the evidence of my misdeeds underneath the dresser hoping no one would notice. A couple of days passed when Mama walked into my bedroom to find me sitting on the floor, scraping away.

"Just what do you think you're doing, young lady?"

"I don't like this furniture and don't want it," I told her.

"That's too bad, because this is all you are getting. You had better stop before I tell your daddy," she warned, "and he tears your bottom from limb-to-limb."

Over the next few days, I permanently scarred both pieces of furniture—front, sides, and top—leaving their appearance looking far worse than before I started. And of course, Mama told Daddy.

"Carrie Jane has taken your welding rods and used them to scratch up her dresser and chest of drawers, because she doesn't like her furniture."

"*Piss, shit, fart!* What a fuckin' little dumb ass. Well, if she wants to tear up her crap, why the hell should I care?"

"You mean you're *not* going to whip her?" Mama asked, as if flustered over his reaction.

"Hell no, I didn't pay for that shit. Good damn thing I didn't, 'cause then I'd stomp her sorry ass," Daddy replied. "At least Dylan's got enough gawddamn sense not to mess up his stuff."

While Dylan did not destroy his furniture, he could do just about anything to me and get away with it, taking advantage of his position as the eldest and only son. He offered daily challenges by drawing an imaginary line with the toe of his shoe onto the worn red, black, and white star-patterned linoleum covering the hallway floor (separating our two bedrooms) daring me to cross over a portion of the seven-foot long territory he claimed to be his. The hallway's unpainted drywall looked as damaged as my furniture, with its scuffs and tears, reflecting a battle-weary stronghold where conflicts started and wars were brought to an end. It was where Dylan took his stand, with hands on hips, like the great Mongol conqueror Genghis Khan. If I should ever be so brave as to accept his challenge and cross the imaginary line, he would humble my lack of respect for his superiority by punching me in the stomach or back. And no matter how many times he beat me up, Mama ignored it.

Then one day something happened, and even she could not overlook his spoiled rotten behavior.

***

Grammy purchased four cutout cloth patterns of Flintstone cartoon characters. She stitched around the fabric's outer edge—with the outside of the pattern facing inward—then pulled the material right-side out through a small opening she left at the bottom to push their stuffing of shredded foam inside before sewing them shut. While Grammy called them *"dolls"*, they were actually pillows with heads. She gave Dylan a Barney Rubble and his son Bamm-Bamm, while I received Barney's wife Betty and Pebbles Flintstone.

One evening, Dylan decided to challenge my Betty and me to a hallway duel. While holding Barney, he took his foot and once more drew his imaginary line across the floor.

"I'll bet you won't walk across this line with Betty," he dared us.

"Betcha we will," I said, stepping forward.

"You think you're so smart," Dylan snorted, while contorting his face at me. "Well, I'll show you. My Barney can beat up your Betty."

"*Can - - not!*"

"Can, too!"

"He cain't because, because . . . my Betty is *bigger* than your Barney!"

Dylan looked down at his Barney. His face grew auburn as he realized that my Betty was indeed larger than his Barney. His blue eyes flickered rapidly in his head, and I knew he was trying to devise a way to pay me back for the truth and still punish me for crossing his line. At loss for a vocal defense, Dylan did the only thing he could think of to regain control: He struck Betty with his Barney several times, as I held her in my arms.

"See," said Dylan as he stepped away from us, "Barney beat up your Betty!"

"He did not!"

"Yes, he did!" Dylan stood laughing, as if pleased with his victory.

"Oh, yeah?"

I could feel the blood rushing to my own face, knowing that once more Dylan had outmaneuvered me. Anger swept over me in a vengeful, uncontrollable wave. I lunged forward and began to pound Dylan's Barney with my Betty.

"Betty beat up Barney, Betty beat up Barney," I chanted proudly in Dylan's face. "*Nah, nah—nah, nah, nah,* Betty beat up Barney!"

Dylan's complexion became awash in purple tones as he dropped Barney to the floor. His fists were clinched into hard, white knots by his side. Air hissed from his nostrils. Instead of striking me with his hands, Dylan released his fists and snatched Betty from my arms and began to pound her repeatedly about my head and shoulders.

"*Give me back my Betty!*" Only the cushioned blows to my mouth muffled my screams.

Then those unwritten childhood rules of engagement shifted; our established battle lines unraveled, sending us into a different dimension. Without warning, Betty's head severed at her neck, grew imaginary wings, and flew inside my bedroom's doorway. Dylan did not allow this minor inconvenience to stop him. He continued striking me with the now lifeless Betty Rubble until her insides burst open, and all he had left in his hands was the cloth that made up her body.

Soft white bits of foam, like snow, fluttered about us and blanketed the floor. Dylan took the printed cloth and wiped the stuffing from his eyes, so he could get a better view of his destruction.

"Har, har, har," he roared. "It looks like your Betty has beat you up and got the stuffing knocked out of her!"

"*I hate you, Dylan Raymond Brine!*" I screamed.

Kneeling to the floor, I attempted to gather up all of Betty's insides, but there was just too much shredded foam. I collected her head and cradled it in my arms.

"Oh, my poor little Betty, did he hit your soft spot? That's okay, Grammy will put you back together, and you'll be good as new."

My remarks caused Dylan to laugh even harder. It was about that moment Mama appeared in the hallway.

"*Wha...?*"

Mama's mouth froze open as if she had just come across some strange horror only witnessed on battlefields. As she peered over the remains of Betty Rubble—Dylan still holding the incriminating evidence in his hands—it felt as though he had actually killed her.

"*What have you done, Dylan?*"

"But . . . but Mama, it's Carrie Jane's entire fault; she made me do it. She stepped over my line and said her Betty could beat up my Barney, because her doll was bigger, so I took her Betty and . . ."

"Shut up, Dylan! I can *see* what you've done."

When Mama regained her composure, for once she did not blame me. All of his pouting and blaming me for what happened, insisting that I just plain bothered him, did not sway her decision. Then she made us clean up every bit of that mess. Despite my own pleas that Betty was salvageable, she was thrown into the garbage with her stuffing. After Mama told Daddy, he whipped Dylan so hard with his black leather belt I thought Dylan's stuffing might come out of him. Then Daddy did something else: He took away Dylan's Barney and Bamm-Bamm, and they were never seen, again. And though I was involved in the fray, I was absolved of any wrongdoing and allowed to keep my Peebles.

And then for a fraction of a second, I faded into the scenery.

CHAPTER 5

Running Away

S upper was ready and growing cold on the kitchen stove. Daddy had left us earlier that Saturday and said he was going out for a bit, which translated into drinking alcoholic beverages at Paw's garage. Most evenings we ate supper without him—be it weekend or weeknight. If Daddy ever arrived in time to join us at the dinner table, it meant he was experiencing a drop too much; well-oiled if a couple of hours later; but after midnight, he stumbled over the threshold pickled and stewed to the gills. I didn't mind when he missed supper, because Daddy usually became upset about something, and he ended up yelling at or striking Dylan and me from across the table.

"Sit up straight, before I kick that gawddamn chair out from underneath you!"

"You'd better eat that shit on your plate, before I knock yer gawddamn teeth down your throat!"

"If you're gonna eat like a fuckin' pig, then I'll buy ya a gawddamn trough!"

Things were different at mealtime after Dinah came to live with us. Mama refused to feed anyone else until the baby had been fed. This simple act took what seemed like forever, because Dinah was a picky eater, spitting out more formula than she swallowed. By the time Dylan and I were served, our own food had grown tacky and tasteless, turning us into picky eaters.

I felt hungrier than usual that particular Saturday evening and thought maybe Mama would let me have something to nibble on before supper, if I asked her real nice.

"Mama, can I have one of your biscuits to eat, please?"

"No, I've got to feed Dinah first, and then you can eat," she replied. "Besides, it will spoil your meal."

"No, it won't, Mama. I promise to eat everything on my plate like a good girl," I begged, eagerly bouncing up and down with my hands clasped in a prayerful plea. "Please, I'm *soooo* hungry."

"I said *no*, Carrie Jane. Now, go sit yourself down and be quiet. I'll feed Dylan *and you* in a little bit."

"S'not fair," I whined, scuffing a shoe along the floor in disgust.

"What in the hell '*s'not fair*'?"

Daddy had opened the front door and stood scraping some dried mud from his cowboy boots by use of our wooden threshold.

"Carrie Jane wants to eat something before supper, and I told her she would have to wait until Dinah's been fed."

Mama's response was directed more towards Dinah, as she wiped away the milk spewing forth from the baby's mouth.

"*Wee--ll*, it looks like you are just shit-out-ov-luck there, Carrie Jane. You'll have to wait and eat like the rest of us. Ain't that right, Dylan?"

Daddy turned to Dylan, who was already seated at the dinner table waiting to be fed. He sat silently with his hands tucked underneath his thighs and legs dangling over the chair seat, avoiding any eye contact with Daddy.

"What's that you said, Dylan? I don't believe I heard your gawddamn answer."

(Sometimes, Daddy picked a fight with Dylan for no sound reason—especially after he had been drinking.)

Daddy stomped passed me in the direction of the table, still wearing his cowboy boots. Dylan shrugged his shoulders.

"That had better gawddamn well mean *yes sir*, you, *you little . . .*"

"*But Daddy, I'm hungry,*" I interrupted, running up to him and tugging at his pant leg. By the scowl that crossed Daddy's face, I could tell that I had just said and done too much.

"Look here, ya little shit, if you don't shut that gawddamn mouth of yours, I'll beat your sorry ass and send you off to bed without anything to eat!" Daddy leaned over and exhaled his smoky, beer-scented breath into my face. "Do you understand me, Carrie *Little Miss Fuckin' Priss* Jane?"

His words stung hard in the back of my throat, so I could not speak. I released his pants leg and stepped back trying not to cry.

"So? What's your gawddamn answer? Huh?"

Now, to a five year old there is no spatial perception between the immediate and long-term consequences of one's speech or actions. No one ever referred to me as *the brightest bulb in the pack,* but one might say I was more like the obstinate bulb that refused to come out of a light socket—the one that snapped off in your hand where the glass met the bulb's base, leaving you cursing and screaming as you pried out the screw thread contact. And you had best remember to turn off the electricity before starting.

"I'll," my voice cracked, "I'll run away!"

"A little chicken shit like you?" Daddy laughed. "I don't believe you've got the gawddamn nerve or sense to go any-*fuckin'*-where by yourself."

"Will so leave. I'll show you. I'll pack my stuff and go."

"*Wee--ll,* if you don't like the way things are done around here then get your ass outta my house, you little stubborn shit. See if anyone misses you, because I sure as hell won't."

Mama briefly looked up from where she was feeding Dinah at the dinner table. Her face remained expressionless and her voice flat as she spoke to Daddy:

"Tell Carrie Jane that she can't take any of her clothes, because Dinah will be able to wear them in a few years."

She looked back to Dinah and ignored me.

"Well, you heard her. Looks like you cain't take your clothes, so what in the hell are you gonna do now—run around naked when the ones you're wearing rot and fall off?" Daddy chuckled as he sat down in his vinyl rocker.

"I'll . . . I'll take my toys and my clown!"

"Take your gawddamn toys. Nobody gives a piss about your fuckin' worn-out shit."

With no real plan in mind of where to go or what to do, I ran into my bedroom to collect my things. Perhaps on my journey (I thought) some nice family would take me in, not call me terrible names or beat me until I was unable to sit down and feed me supper. Through my bedroom walls, I overheard that Daddy was as hungry as the rest of us.

"Irene, aren't you done feeding that baby? I ain't waitin' much gawddamn longer."

"She's almost fed, Billy Ray. It will take me just a couple more minutes until she's burped."

"Well, if it takes much longer, I'll go back to my daddy's and drink beer for my gawddamn supper!"

I grabbed a small burlap bag Grammy had sewn together for me. On one side, she had embroidered an oversized puppy's face with blue thread and a kitten's face with red thread. Cramming most of my few worldly possessions inside (two metal tea sets, three coloring books, a box of crayons, two baby dolls, and a teddy bear), I pulled the bag's drawstrings closed, cradled my orange-haired stuffed clown under my right arm and walked from my bedroom towards the kitchen's backdoor, dragging the burlap bag behind me because its weight was too much for my five-year-old frame to carry. At that moment, as I stood staring at the backdoor, I wanted someone to ask me to stay.

"Okay . . . I'm leaving."

Still seated at the table, Mama said, *"Bye,"* never once looking up from Dinah.

Daddy walked into the kitchen to collect a beer from the refrigerator.

"So? What in the hell are you waiting for?" he asked me. "You wanted to leave so gawddamn bad, then get the fuck outta here, so we can eat supper. Or do you need my ten-and-a-half EE kicked up your ass-side to help you move faster?"

The threatening words he spoke and the lack of concern in Mama's voice made me realize why I did not want to stay. I opened the backdoor (still dragging my burlap bag behind me), climbed down the back steps, and started walking across the backyard headed for the woods; there were houses and people said to be living somewhere on the other side. And if I walked off into the woods, Daddy would never find me, or at least that became my way of thinking. Though slow moving, I was running away from home.

Dylan, who had remained extraordinarily quiet throughout my latest ordeal, decided to get himself up from the table just to shout something frightening at me from the back step.

"Hey dummy, I wouldn't go that way if I were you. The boogeyman lives in those woods."

There I was, halfway across the backyard and earnestly heading for the tree line, only to hear that the boogeyman had moved from Great-Aunt Sophie's ditch and into the woods. I couldn't take the chance of encountering the boogeyman, because Mama might not save me from him a second time. She had Dinah to look after. But I couldn't go back into the house, because Daddy would beat me with his belt and call me ugly names for my stubborn behavior.

"I'll give her a gawddamn boogeyman," Daddy yelled from inside the house.

Standing alone in the backyard, I wondered many things. What did Daddy mean about giving me a *boogeyman*? Which direction should I travel next? Who would take me in? Who would feed me? And again, what did Daddy *mean* about giving me a boogeyman? Then the answer came to me: *Go to Grammy and Paw's house.* Sometimes they let me spend the weekends with them and sometimes during the weekdays. They might even let me live there, if I asked them real nice. Turning around, I headed for the roadway.

Now, for some reason (known only by North Carolina's highway department) someone stopped laying asphalt the other side of *Shit Creek*, a little over a mile down the road from us. As a vehicle rounded a bend in the road, they suddenly ran out of pavement, causing the vehicle to lunge forward and drop several inches into a void exceeding yesteryear. It was as if they forgot that anyone existed beyond that point. For nearly two miles (until you reached Highway 62) there was nothing but a stretch of dirt road with no name, which once served as a horse-and-buggy path for the locals. Moving forward in time, motorized conveyances rumbled past our house—creating dust clouds that drifted long after they disappeared from sight—in search of civilization.

As I stepped onto that road's dirt and gravel surface, my feet wobbled on loose rock. My burlap bag snagged onto some of them. With each step, my toys seemed more of a burden than a comfort. Then it occurred to me, the simplest way to walk my mile journey would be along the shoulder of the road. The burlap bag glided smoothly over the grass as I continued my way to what I hoped would be my new, permanent home.

"Going to Grammy and Paw's house," I sang.

A warm April breeze stroked my cheeks. I took in a deep breath of the freedom-filled air surrounding me. My mind drifted. It felt odd to think that I would no longer live with those people inside that small white-painted box they called a house. They could no longer hurt me or say terrible things to me. Dylan could only torment me when he visited Grammy and Paw. And I discovered that making my own decisions was fun—almost like being a big girl.

My train of thought was broken by the sound of a fast approaching vehicle. I looked over my left shoulder to see Daddy's white pickup truck coming up the road. The truck fishtailed as it slid to a stop along side of me, kicking up dust and rock from underneath its tires and causing me to instinctively jump backwards into a ditch. A flying rock missed me, but as Daddy leaned over the cab and flung open the passenger-side door, its edge struck my right arm, causing me to drop my clown onto the grass and dirt. I was too afraid to feel any pain.

"Get your ass in this truck, Carrie Jane," he hollered at me.

"No, Daddy, I'm running away to Grammy and Paw's house."

"I'll be gawddamn! If you're doin' any running away shit, you'll do it how in the hell I tell you to."

My feet froze, unable to move forwards or backwards. I had a plan, and Daddy was not a part of it. Where would Daddy take me? What would he do to me? I could not make myself get inside his truck.

"No, Daddy," I pleaded, "I don't want to go with you."

"You'd better get your sorry, no-good-for-nothin' ass inside this truck right now, because if I have to get out, I'll beat the *ever-lovin'* shit outta you right here in the middle of the gawddamn road!"

"But you said I could leave and . . ."

"Did you really think I would let you leave and go anywhere you fuckin' pleased? *Huh?* You've got to be the gawddamn dumbest child I've ever seen if you would believe that kinda shit. Now, you'd better damn-well do as I say if you know what's good for you!"

Looking to the road ahead of me and back to Daddy's truck, my first thought involved running as fast as I could in any direction, leaving my clown and toys behind. My second thought saw Daddy catching up with me—either on foot or by truck—and beating my backside unrecognizable. It seemed I had no choice in the matter but to do as he said. My will belonged to Daddy.

Standing in the ditch at the side of the road, the truck's step met me at shoulder level. I picked my clown off of the ground and placed it onto the floorboard. The burlap bag proved too heavy as I attempted to hoist it inside the truck. It slipped out of my arms and fell to the ground. I lifted it a second time, still unable to push it over the threshold plate.

"Ga-a-w-w-d-damnit!"

Daddy leaned over the truck's front bench seat and snatched the bag from me. He flung it to the floorboard like a sack of old potatoes.

"Now crawl your scrawny ass up into this truck."

"Where are we going?"

"You'll find out gawddamn soon enough. Shut up and get in!"

I had barely climbed over the threshold plate and onto the floorboard before Daddy slammed the door to and drove off. For a brief moment, I remained hunched over the bag of toys, supported only by my hands and knees . . . afraid to move . . . afraid Daddy might strike me.

"Get your ass into that fuckin' seat! You ain't riding in my gawddamn floorboard!"

There was one thing I was learning at an early age when it came to Daddy's instruction: Don't make him tell you something twice, or else he would strike you. I crawled up onto the bench seat.

Not a word was spoken between us as Daddy turned left onto Highway 62 and sped off into the countryside, in the opposite direction of Grammy and Paw's place. Unknown houses, tobacco fields, and pastureland raced by my window as he drove faster and faster towards some unknown destination. Fear swept over me as he turned down a lonely stretch of road I had never been on before. The truck skidded off of the pavement onto its shoulder. Trees surrounded us on both sides with nothing but asphalt ahead and behind us. Daddy reached for the passenger's side handle and flung the door open.

"You think you're so gawddamn smart wanting to run away, then there you go: *run away*. Now, get the hell outta my truck! And make sure you take all of that *shit* with you!"

It was different when I was making my own decisions, because I knew where I was and where I was going. Only nothing there looked familiar to me. My little legs hung over the edge of the seat, unable to move me forward. Tears swelled up in my eyes. *I was lost.*

"Please, no . . . Daddy, I'll be a good girl . . . I'll mind Mama."

"Naw, it's too damn late for that shit. You either get out right this gawddamn minute, or I'll knock your ass out onto the ground myself."

I slipped down into the floorboard, then slid over the threshold plate, and stood on the road's grassy edge. Looking around me, I became submerged in the fear of what I did not know. Where was I going to go? What was I going to do? New tears blurred my eyes, so I could no longer see the inside of the truck or Daddy's face.

"I'll be good, Daddy. Please don't leave me here," I begged. *"I'll be good!"*

"I said for you to get your shit outta my floorboard, so I can shut the damn door and get back home to eat my supper before dark. Besides, we don't want you around anymore, because you're nothing but a gawddamn pain in the ass. We have another little girl now, so why in the *fuck* would we need you? You don't mind worth a shit, anyway."

Standing in the middle of my nowhere, I began to tremble—tears streaming down my face. I rapidly sucked in short gasps of air until my lungs felt as if they might burst. Hysteria took over as I suddenly cried out to Jesus, Daddy, and anyone else who would listen to me.

"Please don't leave me! I promise I'll never be bad again!"

"I've a mind to just leave your pitiful, sorry ass out here and let the wild animals have a go at ya."

That was too much. Piercing screams of terror shot from my mouth as I imagined beasts coming from the woods and tearing my body apart, only to have the boogeyman dragging my remains off into oblivion.

"*Aah! No, Daddy, no! Aaah! Aaaah!*" I wailed on and on, screeching at the top of my lungs.

If Daddy spoke for the next several seconds, his voice was drowned out by my own. If he reached over and slapped me, I did not feel it. If he drove off and left me standing there covered in my own snot, I did not see it. Then I grew too exhausted to continue and stood there gasping for air through the flood of tears and mucous.

"*Wee--ll*, if I let ya come back, I'll have to whup your sorry ass as soon as we get home, because you're such an ornery little shit. Then you'll have to go to bed without your supper. And you'll, also, have to do what your momma says and keep your gawddamn mouth shut unless spoken to. You understand me?"

"I'll be a good girl," I sputtered out.

"Then shut the fuck up and get back in the truck!"

I crawled into the truck and onto the seat before Daddy changed his mind. The ride back seemed shorter than from when we left. Perhaps it was because I knew what was waiting for me once we returned. And then I realized Daddy had once more become my boogeyman. Unlike the one in the ditch or in the woods behind us— who manifested in your imagination and nightmares as a scary, invisible monster—Daddy was real. I feared him more at that moment than anything my mind could create.

Only Dylan spoke to me as we walked back into the house, with me still carrying my clown and dragging my burlap bag of toys.

"What's the matter, Carrie Jane? Are you chicken—afraid to run away?"

"Shut your gawddamn mouth, Dylan, or I'll beat your ass as well!"

Before I realized what was happening, Daddy had taken off his belt and started lashing me across my backside. My bag and clown fell to the living room floor. Despite the several past whippings I had received in my five short years, none were as memorable as this particular one. He grabbed onto my left shoulder to stop me from jumping every time the belt came in contact with my flesh. But as the belt slapped over-and-over again across my buttocks and legs, I collapsed onto the floor; it was as if the belt rendered them useless. Daddy's rhythm remained uninterrupted as he snatched me up under my left arm and lifted me into the air. The belt flapped against my lower back; and then again; and again. Screams of pain now replaced those of my earlier terror. This was what it felt like to be devoured by the boogeyman. With one final wallop, he dropped me back to the floor.

"If you ever pull another stupid, fuckin' stunt like that again, I'll put your stubborn ass in the gawddamn hospital. Now pick this shit up and go to bed!"

Sitting there on the floor I held my breath, refusing to exhale. I couldn't move, because the sensation of what it felt like to be in severe pain swept over me, as if someone had peeled away the outer layers of my skin exposing every nerve ending from my back to the soles of my feet. And when I could no longer hold it inside, the air escaped me.

"*Owwww!*" I cried out—tears streaming down my face.

Pushing myself up off of the floor, I grabbed for my discarded clown, barely mustering the strength to drag him into my bedroom. As we crawled into bed, the bag of toys sailed over my head, bursting open and scattering about the floor.

"I thought I told you to pick your shit up! Next time I'll throw it out across the gawddamn front yard!"

This was the first time I discovered if I rolled back and forth on my bed it would ease some of the discomfort from one of Daddy's whippings. Pressing the clown into my chest, we rolled together while I screamed. A moment later, Daddy stood in the hallway and punched his fist against a wall.

"You shut that shit up right now, or else I'll make you sure as hell wish you had!"

Placing the clown over my mouth, I used him to muffle my cries so Daddy could not hear me. That old clown held my tears that night—some from pity, some from fear, but mostly from pain. He soon dried, but the bruises and lacerations on my body remained for several days. The lesson I would take with me from this misadventure was that no matter how hungry, I would never again ask Mama for something to eat before she served us supper.

The desire to run away, though, would never leave me.

CHAPTER 6

Homes Sweet Homes

It began as one of Daddy's rare Sunday afternoon family outings, when he took us to call on some of the locals. Football season had ended, and no stock car races, roller derby or wrestling matches were being broadcast that day, so the only things left on television for him to watch—while drinking his beer—was a golf tournament and reruns of movie musicals. Daddy said that *"only gawddamn sissies play golf,"* and *"men who dance about in women's tights are nothing but fuckin' quares,"* and he would not waste his day off looking at either one of them.

His first stop that afternoon would be to Paw and Grammy's, over on Highway 62. Like most Sundays, Paw had gone fishing, so we visited with Grammy.

***

Daddy told us that in the 1930s, Paw paid seven hundred dollars cash for their three-acre property and a four-room shack, with the revenue he earned off bootlegging and building moonshine stills for his own daddy, Luther Raymond Brine. Then came World War II. Paw closed up their house and moved Grammy, Daddy and Uncle Johnny to Virginia to serve his country by building naval vessels in the Norfolk Naval Shipyards. At the end of the War, they returned home to find parts of the shack had collapsed during their absence.

Now, Paw believed in saving his money and paying cash for everything. Daddy often joked that his tightfisted father *"could squeeze a nickel 'til the buffalo shit in his hand."* With their place falling to the ground, though, Paw had no choice but to take the money he earned from working the shipyards and immediately began building a new house on that same piece of property; only the rains washed away the footings. On a hunch, Paw removed the engines from the abandoned vehicles he kept parked on his three acres, placed them inside deeper holes dug out for the footings, and then covered the engines with concrete. His idea worked, and the house was completed and mortgage free by 1948.

Aside from Paw's structural *enhancements*, some of the house's features reflected that era's post-war design: a functional, well-constructed, one-story box containing three bedrooms, one bath, an eat-in kitchen, laundry room, living room, den, basement, and three *very* small bedroom closets. Dark-brown stained exterior doors (locked by skeleton keys) closed the red brick structure when no one was at home; otherwise, cast-iron squirrels served as door stoppers to prop open the heavy, wooden gateways—even on hot summer nights. Mill-finish, three-sectional storm doors—with a stationary upper glass portion, a center sliding glass insert concealed by a screen and decorative scroll grille, and a lower aluminum panel that served as a kick plate—thinly veiled them from the outside world. An oversized porch wrapped around its front and on one side. The porch's floor was made of smooth, wooden planks that had been hand-painted a shiny grey. Squared redbrick pillars, accented with tan-colored bricks, stood along the porch's edge every six feet to support the weight of its roof. There were no railings installed to prevent you from falling several feet to the ground, which made great fun for rambunctious children.

"*Dylan! Carrie Jane!* You two had better stop that foolishness. I don't want to catch either of you leaping off that porch, again. You could break a leg or worse. Don't make me have to get up and come out there!"

Grammy screamed hollow words in our direction, as she spied on us through a storm door from her recliner in the den; she seldom got up, but then she weighed three hundred pounds.

Dylan and I started at one end of the porch running full speed, with arms outstretched from our sides like airplanes taking off from a runway. As we reached the end we hurled ourselves into the air, only to crash-land on the grass and dirt ground below. The sprained ankles, skinned knees, and bruised backsides seemed worth this sadistic experience, because for a brief moment we could *f l y*.

While the porch filled our entertainment needs, the basement to their house proved just the opposite . . . at least for me. A crumbling staircase—littered with chunks of broken concrete and dead leaves—led to a doorway that rested at the bottom of the unearthed pit. Cinder blocks served as the staircase's two underground outer walls, while the house's bricks extended into the ground to form the inner stairwell wall. Like the porch, there were no railings to prevent you from accidentally plunging over the lip of the outer cinder block walls that surfaced just a few inches above ground level. Crashing down onto *that* staircase was never a flight Dylan or I cared to experience— deliberately or by accident.

When it rained, the waters stood patiently outside the basement door's threshold, as if waiting for someone to let it inside. But Paw left that door bolted, hoping no one would attempt to go in from the outside. Maneuvering those broken steps was too dangerous he warned us.

We entered the basement through an inside hallway door and then down a flight of steep wooden stairs, *without* handrails. Adults balanced themselves by bracing their hands against the floor joists until they could no longer reach them. Sober adults could navigate themselves safely to the bottom step, while children had to crawl down backwards or leap onto the concrete floor below for fear of losing balance and falling. Overhead hung a solitary bulb and pull chain—attached to a double-braided electrical cord—that created fragmented waves of light and darkness as it swung back and forth when lit. Its concrete floor was cluttered with machine parts and tools, as Paw never threw away anything, believing that one day it might, once again, prove to be useful.

Off by itself—in an isolated corner of the dank basement—sat an oversized oil-burning furnace. Though it slept six months out of the year, Paw reawakened it when the fall days turned cool by a single match, to light a fire within its belly. Blue flames hissed from behind a dark glass pane, waiting to consume anyone who stood too close into a pile of ash (or so I feared). Even though Paw extinguished the flame every spring, I reasoned within myself the furnace was even more dangerous if disturbed during its sleep, believing it could rekindle its own flame. I kept a great distance between me and it the times I went down into the basement. After all, a child's imagination can create any unseen horror, but especially when an adult contributes to that fear.

***

It happened about a week after Dinah came home from the hospital. I was spending the day with Grammy when who should appear, but Great-Aunt Ruby. She had crept over for a visit, while Paw and Daddy were still working in Chapel Hill.

"I done hear tell a dead man's buried under yer middle bedroom," Ruby told Grammy, *"and his spirit's livin' down there. Ya know how sensitive I am to those sorta things; I can feel his presence just sittin' in this here chair, and he's none too happy about how he ended up under your house. I'd stay away from that thar basement if I were you, or somethin' turrible's bound to happen."*

Their middle bedroom sat over the crawlspace. Even though there was an outside access door to that area, a section of the cinder block wall that separated the basement from the crawlspace had been chiseled away. The jagged opening was large enough for a grown man to enter by, and he would be directly underneath the middle bedroom. When the crawlspace vents were opened, rays of light streamed through, casting veiled shadows into every corner and forming obscure images across the earthen floor. It was enough to frighten the bejeezus out of little children *and* susceptible adults.

When Grammy told Paw of Ruby's macabre tale, he became furious.

"Good god, woman, can't you see that damned evil sister of yours is making up that nonsense? For some sick-ass reason, Ruby's been trying her damn-level best to drive you crazy over the years. And I wouldn't be surprised to learn that her son-of-a-bitch husband

Chester put her up to that. They are both jealous that you live in a nicer house than they do. I suspect all of this bullshit is about money. And I'd better not find out she's been coming over here while I'm away, or I'll be paying her another damn visit."

When Grammy refused to even go into her own hallway near the basement door, I figured the story must be true and told Daddy. He said that I was as *"stupid"* as Grammy to believe that *"horseshit,"* because Ruby was *"nuttier than a gawddamn fruitcake."*

Next door, though, separated from their house by a small patch of woods were Mills Methodist Church, its parsonage, and a cemetery. So, I reasoned within myself that somebody mistook their land for the graveyard before Paw built their house and buried the man there by mistake; only Ruby swore to Grammy she heard the man under the middle bedroom was somebody Paw did not like.

Then Dylan took to taunting me.

"Chicken," he called me. "I dare you to run down into the basement, look through that hole in the wall, and ask if there is anybody at home."

Despite my fears, I was always ready to show him how bravely stupid I was by accepting one of his ridiculous challenges.

"Oh, yeah? Well . . . well . . . just watch me!"

Crawling my way backwards down the steep flight of wooden basement steps, then sidestepping the furnace like a frightened mouse for fear it might awaken and devour me, I ran as fast as I could to the wall's opening. Standing on tiptoes, I leaned inside the gaping hole, catching the musty odor of decaying soil in my nostrils. With my heart pounding in my chest from an unforeseen terror, I screamed out:

"*Is there anybody home?*"

I wasted no time waiting around to see if a boney hand reached out of the ground and grabbed me. Crawling as fast as I could back up the staircase, I always managed to fall—facedown—ramming my right shin into the edge of a wooden step and leaving me with a nasty scrape and permanent scar. The peculiar thing about this was that it always happened on the same step and on the exact same spot of my shin every time. Refusing to believe it occurred because I was a clumsy child, I imagined the dead man's ghost was underneath those steps tripping me as I ran upstairs, as his way of inviting me to come back when I could stay longer. As I continued my breathless journey towards the landing, Dylan always stood there mocking me.

"*Fraidy-cat!*" he called me.

When I finally got up the nerve to ask Dylan why he never ventured down into the basement alone, he scoffed at me and said, "I'm not stupid."

***

Back from the highway a bit, the other side of Paw and Grammy's brick house, stood what was left of the original four-room shack. It sat isolated on a slight hill, like a condemned building that was ready to give way to its deterioration. Daddy and Uncle Johnny were small boys when they first moved there. Both told a story of how the previous owners had left the floors covered in animal feces, only they could never agree as to what kind of animal or how deep.

"They raised chickens in there," Uncle Johnny told us. "And the chicken poop was knee-high up your britches leg."

"Naw, Johnny, they kept these big ole dogs inside," Daddy (being the older brother) corrected him. "There was dog shit two inches deep we had to scrape off those gawddamn floors."

Outside the shack, machine parts and old broken-down automobiles cluttered what was once its front yard. Hundreds of empty Coca-Cola, Pepsi, Nehi, Bubble-Up and Royal Crown Cola bottles lay scattered about. Kudzu covered an outhouse and the climbing vine had even attached itself to some of the shack's dried grey walls on the inside and out. In front of the shack, the remains of what was once a front porch had fallen—crumbled to the ground—so it was impossible to enter by the front door unless you used a ladder to climb over the threshold. You had to go around to the back and enter where the outer kitchen walls had collapsed.

The house remained off limits to us children; Daddy, Mama, Grammy, and *especially* Paw, said so.

"I don't want to catch you children playing around that house. It's too dangerous," he often told us.

Snakes patrolled the area; ticks lived amongst the tall grass and weeds; and poison ivy crept its way around dead wood and tree trunks. Wasps and mud daubers had taken up housekeeping in any available corner they could find. Spiders webbed their way throughout. Glass—from shattered windowpanes—reflected a dull haze off the sunken wooden floorboards that had dry-rotted to the point they could suddenly give way underneath you. Those seemed sound reasons for anyone to stay away and ones that should have made me afraid, but sometimes—when no one was around—I found myself sneaking off to that old shack for a peek at the past.

There I could watch the world around me from behind the remaining smoky windowpanes, but it could not watch me back. What secrets those walls told of days that had long since passed. Holes decorated them where flying objects and angry fists exposed its innermost layer. Leather strap marks and indentions from tools marred areas where little boys had been physically abused by their drunken father. It was there that I realized Daddy and Uncle Johnny were once children.

Uncle Johnny seldom mentioned those awful moments from his youth, and when he did, he treated the matter as if telling a silly joke. He sometimes told a story of how one night he found Paw seated at the kitchen table—*drunk on spirits*—eating his supper.

"I walked in the kitchen and said, '*Hey, Daddy.*' Next thing I knew, he knocked me acrost the room and I slid down the wall like a limp dish rag."

"What did you do?" I asked him, waiting for the punch line.

"I learned to never say, '*Hey, Daddy*' again when I walked into a room," he laughed, his face burning with a red glow that matched the color of his hair.

As for my daddy—Billy Ray—he seldom laughed about Paw's abuse. Daddy told us stories even when he hadn't drunk too much beer, sometimes drifting in and out of the past, as if reliving the moment.

"When I was a boy, my daddy would have me help him at the garage. If I didn't use a gawddamn tool exactly like he'd showed me, he'd beat me with it. I've been whupped with a siphon hose, handsaw, a-square, and thirty-six-inch screwdriver more times than I can remember.

"There's this one time, Daddy comes home after he's been out drinkin' all night, and we're all in bed asleep. He goes to the icebox looking for something to eat.

"A little while later we hear him yell: '*Y'all got any more of this here meatloaf?*'

"Momma hollers from her bed: '*That's not meatloaf; that's the dog's food.*'

"Daddy goes into this gaggin' fit like he's trying to throw the shit back up, so Johnny and I start laughing. Then Daddy comes in and beats the tar outta us—right in our bed. We sure-as-shittin' couldn't walk the next day."

If I stood there in that dilapidated shack long enough, I thought I could almost hear their small screaming voices, pleading for Paw to stop. Or was it the echo of my own voice I heard? Even still, the remnants of that shack stood there, like a memorial to things passed and of things to come.

***

While their brick house was under construction, Paw built a garage where he operated a repair shop. A long dirt and gravel half-circular driveway—with a grassy field in-between—connected the brick house on one side of the property to the garage on the other. The two structures kept a silent watch over one another, like envious siblings who desired something the other had.

A graveyard of rusted automobiles and machine parts continued an uneven path along the half-circle driveway from the shack to the dingy brown, cinder block building that Paw made his living out of. Rusting sheets of tin covered its roof. Tall weeds grew around the garage's exterior. Two enormous wooden slabs— the size of walls—served as sliding entrance doors and each secured by a simple padlock. They were covered with asphalt shingles and hung from once greased tracks. The door that covered its front faced their brick house, with only a small dirt pathway leading to it from the driveway. Junk and weeds cluttered the path's sides. The other door sat against Highway 62, with a small gravel and dirt area for Paw's customers to park. He kept a 1949 Willys "Jeep" truck—with a winch on the back and portable welding machine hitched to the bumper—parked next to the far corner of the building facing towards the roadway when he was open for business. The red-over-white pickup had the head of an Indian chief custom painted across its hood as a reminder of an Indian Motorcycle Paw rode in his younger days. On the truck doors, painted in black stencil lettering were the words: *Brine Portable Welding.*

Paw was a self-employed arc welder, electrician, and mechanic by trade, but an inventor at heart. Though he had long since retired from his bootlegging and *cookin' shine* days, sometimes he took orders for his illegal, custom-made moonshine stills.

Inside the garage he stored Lincoln welders of various sizes, acetylene tanks and torches, welding rods and shields. Daddy, Mama, Grammy, but *especially* Paw, always warned Dylan and me to never look into the light without wearing a face shield or tinted goggles, else we might burn our retinas from the arc flash. Sometimes, I couldn't help but watch the sparks through naked eyes, as they cascaded from the electric arc, created by a welding rod striking against metal— dancing balls of fire extinguishing themselves on the garage's concrete floor beneath Paw's feet.

Alongside of those items were various mechanical contraptions and gadgets Paw had invented from the spare parts of machinery and vehicles he kept littered about his property. Only Paw knew how to operate these contrivances. He would place a broken part into a vice-like object, push on the power button, turn a steering wheel he had removed from a car, move a few more odd-shaped gizmos around, and somehow repaired whatever it was that needed fixing. They were all quite fascinating to watch in operation, but not very pretty to look at.

But, Paw was not without his mechanical masterpiece. He built a small working replica of an old steam locomotive—complete with a smoke stack and whistle. The engineer's cab was just big enough for a child to ride on the back. During select times in the summer and fall, Paw ventured off to old-timey gas and steam engine shows or threshers reunions to display his miniature marvel, and most times he came back with ribbons and prize money. The rest of the year it remained parked inside his garage.

"Hands off—that's not something to play with," he scolded me, the times I took a notion to pet his little toy.

As to be expected, the garage's insides were quite filthy from the dirt and grime that had accumulated over the years. The combined odors of sweat and grease left a lingering smell on anyone who walked inside. Tools and scrapped parts laid scattered about the garage floor and on benches in no particular order, as if happenstance played a part in the decision-making. High on the walls hung outdated calendars of unclad ladies that Paw (unashamedly) refused to take down. A 1940s General Electric refrigerator stood next to the front entrance—most days filled with sodas taken from the stacked wooden crates delivered by the Coca-Cola man. It appeared to have never been cleaned—inside or out—nor had the small icebox ever thawed, but it kept those green-glass, hobble skirt six-and-a-half ounce Coca-Cola bottles icy cold on a hot summer's day.

When I got up the nerve and could take the sting of Paw's voice, I would ask him for one of those sodas. Sometimes he just said, *"No,"* claiming he did not have enough for himself.

"But Paw," I would say without thinking, *"you have all them bottles inside those wooden boxes next to the refrigerator. Why cain't I have one of them?"*

"The damned things are hot, that's why," he would scowl at me. "Now, move your bottom back up to the house, so I can get some work done!"

If in one of his less stingy moods—when he said I could have one—I would test his generosity even further by asking for a pack of those *nabs* from the Lance glass display jar he kept on top of the refrigerator.

"Damn it, if children don't try to eat you out of house-and-home. They won't let you have shit around here. Just go ahead and take every damn thing I got!"

Since I was too small to reach the jar, Paw had to stop his work and get the peanut butter-filled crackers for me, which meant he was none too happy about that. Shoving them towards me with a grease-stained hand

and a *"here,"* I snatched the crackers, uttered a quick *"thank you,"* and ran as fast as my legs would carry me back to their house. They never tasted quite as good as on those extraordinary occasions when he would just offer me the Coca-Cola and nabs without having to ask for them. Those were the times I liked him best, because I figured in his own peculiar way he must have sort of liked me, too.

While Grammy did not approve of me being inside the garage, sometimes she insisted I go there on a special errand.

"Carrie Jane, go down to the garage and ask your Paw for a Coke," she ordered me from her recliner, still clad in her pajamas and puffing on a Benson & Hedges cigarette, watching some afternoon soap opera on the television like *The Guiding Light* or *As the World Turns.* "I've run out and haven't had time to go to the grocery store."

If she had her teeth in, I was to, also, ask for a pack of nabs. But if they were soaking in a cup, she only wanted the soda.

"And while you're there, tell him to give you one as well."

As a child, there were certain things I was just plain scared of: Daddy's belt; the boogeyman; giants; accepting gum from old men in wheelchairs; being left on the side of the road; visiting a dead man underneath my grandparents' house; and oil-burning furnaces. They all ranked at the top of my fear list. Asking Paw if *Grammy* could have one of his Coca-Colas was another.

Standing nervously just inside a doorway to the garage, wringing my little hands together, those were the times I waited to be spoken to.

"*Well?*" Paw would raise his voice in agitation, glancing away from his work at me. "*What do you want?*"

"Um, uh, um . . ."

"Well, say what you have to say, and then leave me alone. Can you not see that I have work to do?"

"Yes'ir, um, Grammy wants, um . . ."

Just the mention of her made Paw stop what he was doing and turn his entire body towards me.

"Your Grammy wants *what*?"

"Um, Grammy wants . . ."

By this point I would be shifting my feet from side-to-side, as if I were about to wet myself, pointing my left hand towards his refrigerator.

". . . Grammy wants one of your Coke colas."

His greying flattop seemed to bristle up like the spines on a porcupine, and the veins on his face rose to the surface, emitting a ruddy-red glow on an otherwise sun-browned complexion. His arms hung down by his sides, while his hands continuously formed and released fists.

"What in the hell makes her think I would give you a soda to take back to her?"

"Grammy said she ain't got none left."

"You tell *Grammy* that I said she needs to get off of her damn lazy butt and do some shopping."

Perhaps I was just a slow, literal child who did not understand unless I was told *yes, you may have one* or *no, you may not have one.* Or perhaps I expected him to give me whatever Grammy wanted.

"So, does that mean she cain't have one? She said for you to give me one, too, and ask for a pack of . . . *nabs*?"

Paw's face drew a blank expression, though his clear blue eyes nearly crossed from staring at me so hard.

"What is the matter with you, child? Do you not understand a gawddamn thing? Hell no, she *'cain't'* have one of my Coca-Colas, and neither can you. Now, get out of my damn garage and leave me alone!"

I didn't stop running until I was back on their front porch. Though he never tried, I wasn't about to wait around to find out if Paw might strike me with one of his tools. Sometimes he acted and sounded just like Daddy.

"Where are my Coke and crackers?" Grammy asked me.

"Paw done said you need to get off your *'lazy butt and do some shopping.'* " Minus the cursing, I always told her his exact response.

"Humph!" she always snorted. "Was he upset?"

"Yes, ma'am."

"Humph!" she snorted a second time, then returned to her cigarette and television program.

As for Mama, she said the garage was no place for young ladies to visit, so it was strictly off limits to me. Not for Dylan, though.

"That's because he's a boy," Mama told me. "And I don't want you showing off around those men."

What she meant by *"showing off"* never made much sense to me, and Mama never bothered to explain when asked, but she warned me to stay away from the garage or else. *Or else*, of course, meant Daddy.

Being a curious child, I found Paw's garage fascinating, and would sneak over there some evenings while Grammy napped in her chair. On occasion, Paw didn't seem to mind if I stayed for a couple of minutes, but most times my presence there just plain irritated him. When the locals came to do business or visit with him, I remained quiet and listened. Some were relatives or his friends who addressed me by name, while others were farmers who nodded or spoke a simple *"Howdy"* to me. Then there were the strangers I had no idea whom they might have been or where they came from. And Paw never made introductions, and sometimes he even asked me to leave, especially when that peculiar farmer from across the highway came calling.

✳✳✳

Jeeter Johnson lived with his *old momma*, Luttie Mae, and step-daddy, Homer Watkins, in a one-and-a-half story white-frame farmhouse nestled behind an ancient Magnolia and scattered Chinaberry trees. Theirs was an uncommon lifestyle, especially during the 1960s. You could say they were downright backwards compared to the rest of us locals—even more so than Great-Aunt Sophie and her *"shit hole."* Daddy called them *"backwoods, Hardshell Baptists"* who moved there some years before *"from over yonder a-ways"* (meaning Forsyth County).

As a child, none of that meant anything to me, because Baptists were just plain Baptists as far as I knew. But he told me there were all sorts of Baptists in this world, like Free Will Baptists, Missionary Baptists, and Southern Baptists. Only those Hardshell Baptists did not believe in going out there and trying to save souls, so the notion of missionary work was a foreign concept to their members.

"Predestined" was a word Daddy used to describe them.

"If you ain't among their *chosen* or *elect* few, they believe there is no way yer sorry ass will ever be saved and go to Heaven, because God done decided a long time ago your one-way ticket was punched for Hell," Daddy explained.

That made me a bit concerned, seeing how we didn't regularly attend any of the area churches: Baptist, Methodist or Quaker. If God hadn't chosen us for salvation, then there was no hope. Daddy told me not to worry much about *"that predestined bullshit,"* as he had his own doubts about the salvation and sanity of those folks living across the road from Paw and Grammy.

They drew their water from a well (using a rope, bucket, and windlass); preferred an outhouse to indoor plumbing; cooked on a wood stove; and they didn't even own a telephone. When Luttie Mae needed to make a phone call, she crossed the highway to use Paw and Grammy's. They drove a pickup truck for church and not pleasure, and owned a tractor for work, as they earned their living by mostly raising tobacco.

When not working in their fields, Jeeter seemed to be in Paw's garage. Many times, I found him sitting there all blank faced on Paw's busted-back cane chair, with his legs crossed like a woman, eating a pack of Paw's nabs and drinking one of his Coca-Colas. He always wore the same old faded-blue overalls, red-and-white-checkered flannel shirt, and oversized brown work boots covered in dried mud, with a full-brimmed, brushed leather hat to cover his balding head. Jeeter never spoke; he just nodded his head towards me to acknowledge my presence—and grunted.

Dylan and I figured Jeeter could not talk, though Paw told us that Jeeter could speak as well as we did; he just didn't have anything to say. We guessed it had something to do with those yearly visits he made to the mental institution in Butner, whenever he "went off," as Daddy called it.

Every time we asked Paw what was the matter with Jeeter, he refused to tell either one of us anything about him. Paw said his problems were none of our business. But Daddy would, especially after he had a few too many beers to drink and was not in a violent way.

"Ever since I can remember that Jeeter's been one *crazy* son-*ov*-a-bitch," Daddy told us. "And so has that old momma of his, Luttie Mae. I've caught her standing behind that big old Magnolia tree in her front yard plenty of times, peeking around the trunk to see what we were doing over there at the house. She must think she's invisible or somethin', because every damn time I'd ask her what she was looking at from behind that tree, she'd say, '*You didn't see me!*'

"And that stupid asshole, Homer, she married, he couldn't walk and chew gum at the same gawddamn time. You could ask him, '*Hey, Homer, how's that tobacco crop comin' in this season?*'

"That dumb bastard would answer you with a, '*Yup, planted a row of turnips this year. Ain't never done that 'fore. Yup, and they's a-growin'.*'

"Shit, the only person out of that fuckin' nutty bunch that ever had a lick of gawddamn sense was Jeeter's real daddy, Leland Johnson, and I'll be damned—back in 48'—if he didn't go off and blow his brains out with a shotgun, right in their front bedroom. And it was that gawddamn Luttie Mae's fault!

"Leland had smoked all of his life and had lung cancer. So, Daddy told Johnny and me to never tell Leland the truth if he asked, because Leland couldn't take knowing he had cancer; Daddy told us to say he had a heart problem, or else he'd take a two-by-four to our backside. Only Luttie Mae decided for some *gawddamned* reason to let him know the truth. Then after telling him, she walked out of the bedroom and into the kitchen to fix supper, and that's when Leland took the shotgun to himself. We all heard the shot since Leland's bed was backed against an opened front porch window. After the funeral, Earl found a piece of Leland's skull in their front yard next to a Chinaberry tree. We went back to his grave, poked a hole in the ground, and buried the rest of him. Leland was a good old man."

Daddy would grow silent for a moment—his face in distress to the point of sadness. But then his brow furrowed, and his teeth clinched as if on edge.

"A few weeks later, Luttie Mae married that piece-*ov*-shit, Homer. She didn't even wait until Leland was cold in the ground," he said, raising his voice in anger. "Anyway, Leland had bought himself a 1948 red Chevy pickup right before he died.

"One day Homer drives the truck over to Daddy's garage and says, '*Come out 'ere and have a-looks at my new truck!*'

"Daddy says back to him, '*Just when in the hell did that become your truck? I was there when it belonged to Leland Johnson!*'

"Daddy has always hated that Homer son-*ov* . . ."

"But Daddy," I would interrupt him, "what about Jeeter? He cain't talk, can he? Paw says he can, but I don't believe it."

"Oh, that crackbrained son-*ov*-a-bitch can talk, all right," Daddy said. "When I was a boy, he'd get so mad at his old momma that he'd lock her outta their house.

"And there'd go Luttie Mae, running back and forth in their front yard like a cackling old hen screaming, '*Jeeter, Jee—ter, you better let me back in that house, ya* hear, 'fore I go call the shur—iff! They'll come and take you away, again. Jeeter . . . Jeeee—ter!'"

Daddy laughed at his mocking version of her shrill voice, as he started to fade away from us into his past.

"Then off Luttie Mae would run acrost the road, with her apron and skirt tail flying up over her knock knees, and baggy bloomers showing, while holding down some gawddamn black wig onto that bald head of hers so it wouldn't fall off.

"'Raymond, I need to use your telly-phone to call the shuriff. Jeeter's done gone off and locked me out of the house, again. Why, I just don't know what I'm to do with that boy, 'cept send him back to the hospital. He's done went and got way too big for me to bring down acrost my knees and give him a good switchin'.'

"When the sheriff arrived, Jeeter would yell from inside the house, 'Ain't lettin' Momma back in!'

"The sheriff would have to kick in the front door and haul Jeeter off to Butner. That son-ov-a-bitch has went off at least once every year since I've known him.

"One time—when I was fourteen or so—Jeeter got into one of his spells and started chasing his old momma around their front yard with a butcher knife. I figured Luttie Mae must've really pissed him off about somethin'. And I'll tell you one more damn thing, that old woman could do some running, while out there screaming at the top of her lungs.

"'Jeeter!'"

Daddy would lean back into his brown vinyl swivel rocker and take a long drag from a cigarette. His eyes faded into a blank stare—unmoving—as one without sight. I imagined he was once again a fourteen-year-old boy standing in his parent's front yard—hands crammed stiffly down into his pants pockets—watching and waiting to see what Jeeter would do next.

"'Jeeter, no Jeeee—ter . . . put that knife down! Help me, Ray—mond! Jeeter's tryin' to kill me! R-a-y-m-o-n-d! Help!'

"I stood there and watched my daddy walk acrost the road and right up to Jeeter.

"'Now, Jeeter,' he says, 'you stop this foolishness, and hand me that knife—right this minute!'

"I was skeered he was gonna cut Daddy, but Jeeter handed him the knife without saying a word. With Jeeter being right much older and bigger than me at the time, there wouldn't have been much I could do about it if he had."

Leaning forward in his chair, Daddy came back to the present, his eyebrows crushed angrily into the bridge of his nose.

"I don't know why Daddy lets that fuckin' nut-bag idiot sit around in his garage all the damned time; he has ever since Johnny and I were boys. And you sure-as-hell better not ever let him hear you making fun of Jeeter, or else he'll knock your ass acrost 62 with whatever he has in his hands. We learnt firsthand to keep our mouths shut about that idiot or at least around my daddy.

"And another thing, I had better not catch either one of you talking to that scary-ass Jeeter-son-ov-a-bitch, because there ain't no tellin' what he might try to do to ya! If I ever hear tell you have, *I'll* kick your little asses so hard, you'll be picking shit out from between your teeth for the next ten years," Daddy warned us.

Paw generally tolerated Jeeter just sitting in his garage for hours on end, never saying a word. A couple of times—when Paw was in one of his more contrary moods—I overheard him tell Jeeter his company would be appreciated elsewhere.

"Isn't it about time for you to go home and help your mother?" Paw sternly spoke at him.

As was his custom of never uttering a word, Jeeter would rise from the chair and lumber across the road, only to return in a few hours, and help himself to more free sodas and crackers.

***

On the other side of Paw's garage sat a one-story, white-framed and brick-accented house. It was a delicate place, surrounded by blooming flowers and trees, and the scent of wild honeysuckle. It was the only house in the area that possessed any real color or life. The three spinster sisters who lived there were just as fragrant. Miss Ruthie, Miss Myra, and Miss Ada Bamberger were among my *most* favorite people during childhood. Born of German Jewish immigrants, their parents chose that area of North Carolina to make their home, not realizing it was inhabited by some serious members of the Ku Klux Klan, whose sole mission was to keep all Catholics, blacks, and Jews out of their sacred territory.

But Paw's daddy, Luther, took a liking to their Jewish father, Samuel Bamberger, and said he did not have a problem with him living in *his* community, giving him the final say-so in the matter. According to Daddy, Mr. Bamberger appreciated the *medicinal properties* of Luther's homebrew.

The Bamberger sisters stood barely four-and-a-half feet tall. When they sat upon a couch or chair, their petite legs dangled over the edge like floating anchors, suspended in air. Silver had taken over what had once been brown hair, and porcelain complexions smoothed out their ageless faces. They were dolls dressed in simple cotton-print frocks, living in a doll's house. They always had a smile on their faces and kind words to say to everyone who visited them.

Sometimes, Paw or Grammy would take Dylan and me to visit their next-door neighbors, but no Halloween passed by without a treat from the Bamberger sisters. And theirs was always the first stop. Hurrying us inside through their back porch, they led us into a spotless kitchen filled with the aroma of freshly baked goods.

"Please, please come into our home," smiled Miss Ruthie.

"My goodness, what pretty little children, and so well mannered," complimented Miss Myra. "Don't you agree, Ada?"

"Oh, yes, Myra, such wonderful little children," Miss Ada acclaimed. "Your parents are so blessed to have two such lovely children. And they must have cake before they go."

As Miss Ruthie was trying to take our coats, Miss Myra and Miss Ada would be bouncing lightly about the kitchen, taking out their best china and silver to serve us a piece of cake, while filling up our paper *trick-or-treat* sacks with all manner of candy and chocolates. Hugs that smelled of rosewater and lilac remained with me for the rest of the evening. It was only with the Bamberger sisters that I felt special as a child.

Since Daddy and Uncle Johnny grew up next door to the Bamberger family, they became well acquainted with the sisters. Daddy often told us how they hugged Uncle Johnny and him when they were little boys and fed them cake. Both swore they were *"the nicest old ladies"* they had ever known. They even introduced the boys to Brazil nuts; only this South American seed went by the offensive name of *Ni - - er Toes*.

"Once, when Johnny and me were about four and five years old, Miss Ruthie, Miss Myra and Miss Ada gave us each a handful of these nuts," Daddy told us. "So, when we finished eatin' 'em, Johnny and I went back to ask for more, only Miss Myra said they had given us their last one. But they had this old colored maid who came in from High Point to help them a couple of days per week. So, I asked them, *'What about her?'* and pointed down at that colored woman's feet. *'You can cut off her toes and give 'em to us.'* That was the funniest damned thing they'd ever heard. Even the old colored maid laughed. Nobody told us those things came out of trees."

Another time, Daddy and Uncle Johnny went to their house for a visit, but on the way, they found what Daddy referred to as *"a big ole worm"* on top of the fence separating the two properties. Instead of stopping to play with it, they rushed to Miss Ruthie to show her what they had found.

"'Oh, my goodness, boys, that's not a worm. It's a spreading adder! Don't you dare get close, because it's a dangerous snake,' she told us and went running back to the house for a hoe.

"I'll bet she chopped that gawddamn thing into a hundred pieces," he laughed. "Johnny and I had the best times growing up with them living next door."

Even as an adult, Daddy enjoyed his visits with the Bamberger sisters. And as he sat on Paw and Grammy's den couch that Sunday afternoon, he announced he would be looking in on the ladies.

"Oh boy, can I go, too, Daddy? Please? Can I go, too?" I asked, hopping up and down in the middle of the den floor, like a jubilant puppy that couldn't wait to go outside, sniff the bushes, and take a wee.

"Hell no, you cain't go!" Daddy then looked to Dylan, who was standing under the arched doorway between the den and kitchen. "And there ain't no use in you asking me either, because you're staying here as well."

Dylan tilted his face towards the floor. He remained silent.

"But Daddy, why cain't we go?"

Tears welled up in my eyes. Why did Daddy not understand? All I wanted was a kind word and a hug from the Bamberger sisters. And though Dylan never spoke, I felt certain he wanted to go, too.

"Because I said you *cain't*! I'm taking your momma and new baby sister to show off, and I don't need the two of you in the way to cause me any damn problems. So, shut your *gawd*-damn trap and do as you're damn-well told."

It was rare that I ever asked Daddy if I could go anywhere with him, because I was just plain afraid of how his response might be delivered. He answered with either a *"Hell no!"* Or he skipped on the verbal exchange and took his belt to me.

"S'not fair, 'cause I wanna go, too," I mouthed back, stamping one of my little girl shoes onto Grammy's den floor.

"What in the hell did you just say to me, you little shit? I'll knock your damned teeth down your throat for talkin' back to me!"

Daddy sprung off of the den couch. As he reached out to grab hold of me, I managed to slip away and run across the den past Grammy, who sat quietly in her recliner—still wearing her pajamas, holding a lit cigarette, and sipping on a bottle of soda. As I stopped at the storm door leading onto the side porch, I looked over my shoulder and noticed Mama had not moved from the couch, but sat quietly holding Dinah in her arms—the baby wrapped inside a pink-and-white receiving blanket. For a brief moment, I imagined this was all Dinah's fault; if she had not been there, I would be the one going on this visit. Angry at Daddy for not letting me go and at Dinah for gaining all of the attention, I slammed the heel of my left hand into the door's sliding-glass insert hoping to push it open, so I could flee outside and run away.

This mill-finish storm door, with its broken latch that never stayed shut, decided on that particular occasion to become stuck. My hand—the hand of a five year old—went through the glass pane, causing it to shatter into pieces and fall onto the floor around me. Stunned, I looked at my left hand to find blood trickling down my arm and dripping onto my clothes and the shards of glass below. A gash had been torn into my left wrist under my thumb. From the shock of this misadventure and the sight of my own blood, I stood there frozen in time, fearfully wondering where life would take me beyond that moment. It did not take Daddy long to decide for me. Lifting me out of the glass by the back of my dress, he stood me in the middle of the den. An event was about to take place that would dwarf any programming on our television that day.

Pulling off the belt worn around his waist, in one fell swoop he doubled the leather strap and began to beat me wildly about the backside of my body—thighs, back, calves, and buttocks—his left hand gripping my left wrist, while extending my left arm over my head to steady me in place.

"Why you sorry-ass excuse for a child," he screamed at me over the lashes, "I'll show you who in the hell is in charge around here. Talk back to me, will ya? And if you ever break another gawddamn door, I'll break every fuckin' bone in your body!"

When he finished the whipping, Daddy dropped me to the floor and agitatedly refitted his belt back through the loops of his jeans. Looking down at his hand he noticed the wet blood—my blood—clinging to his left hand.

"*Well, shit!*" he snarled and began wiping it briskly down the left front leg of his dungarees, as if he had just stuck his hand into a pile of dog poop.

"Now, you had better have this gawddamn mess cleaned up before we get back, or I'll beat your ass a second time," Daddy said, pointing to the glass covered floor. "Irene, let's go."

He pushed open what remained of the storm door and walked outside, with the sound of crunching glass under his feet. Mama followed closely behind carrying Dinah.

Sitting in the middle of the den floor, I watched the blood continue to trickle off of my wrist and into my lap. Of course, I was crying and of course, I was in pain, but I could not decide which hurt me the most: my cut wrist, the whipping, or just plain not being able to visit with the Bamberger sisters.

"You need to go into the bathroom and warsh that cut under the faucet, before it gets infected. There are bandages and alcohol in the medicine cabinet,"

Grammy told me. "If you need to stand on the commode to reach the cabinet, make sure you put the lid down first, else you might fall in."

Though all thumbs, I managed to stop the bleeding and apply an adhesive bandage to the wound. I learned how to sweep and pick up glass fragments, albeit not without sticking myself a few more times with some exceptionally sharp pieces.

Days later, I imagined it was that ole dead man buried under Paw and Grammy's house who caused the door not to open; he must have been standing on the other side holding it shut, trying to pay me back for all of the times I'd been down in the basement disturbing his eternal sleep. In the future, it seemed wise to ignore Dylan's silly challenges, and leave the unknown alone.

Come Halloween, though, I would get my visit with the Bamberger sisters.

CHAPTER 7

Any Port in a Drunken Storm

When I was growing up, most of my world appeared black and white and grey—sort of like the movies and television programs from the early 1960s. What little color that surrounded me was green, but the shade was often muted, so one could easily mistake it for a murky grey. Those who lived around us (with the exception of the Bamberger sisters) rarely planted flowers or blooming plants, and the farmers only raised crops. The suckers, which grew from the tops of tobacco plants, were the only plant life that added a third dimension to the area's landscape before the farmers lopped them off. And it seemed every farmer or wealthy landowner dug a pond on their property—some stocked with fish—and surrounded it with cattle and a barbed wire fence. These waters blended into the green and black and white and greyness of what I saw, as pond scum covered their

129

surface, so those who dared enter the stagnant waters could never see what might be lurking beneath them.

Five months after the birth of Dinah, Daddy altered his Saturday ritual of going to Paw's garage: the seventh-day gathering place where menfolk surrendered all of their commonsense into an inebriated state. Instead, he told Dylan and me to put on our swimsuits, because Paw and he were going to take us to a local pond to go swimming.

Mama did not approve.

"Billy Ray, I don't know if that's such a good idea. Dylan and Carrie Jane are still pretty small and neither one of them know how to swim," Mama argued. "And these ponds aren't the cleanest things for children to be playing in."

"They're my young'uns', too, so I'll do whatever in the hell I please with them," he informed her. "And I'll have you know this pond we're taking them to ain't as filthy as most; it doesn't have all of that shit floating on top."

Mama's voice stilled.

Paw arrived that morning in his new 1965, green-over-white Ford pickup truck, with his Crestliner Voyager boat and trailer hitched to the truck's rear bumper.

"Come on and get in," he shouted to us. "This daylight is burning, and we need to stop off at Hinson's Store before we reach Jennings Pond!"

Climbing inside the new truck, I smelled beer. Paw held an opened bottle between his legs. I looked back to see Mama standing alone in our doorway, shivering—arms crossed tightly against her chest as if concealing herself against an imaginary cold wind blowing in from the south. Her eyebrows crushed together, meeting at the bridge of her nose, giving off a look of despair. Her facial expression riled Daddy.

"Gawddamnit, Irene, we're just taking them to the fuckin' pond!" he yelled at her.

Paw laughed. "Get in, Billy Ray."

"But Daddy," my daddy snorted through his nostrils as he slammed the truck door shut, "every blasted thing I do, she's either running off at the gawddamn mouth or giving me one of those *you shouldn't be doing that* damn looks. Cain't do shit without her bitchin' about it."

"That's how women are most of the time," Paw chuckled. "I stopped listening to your mother years ago. It was the only way I could put up with her."

***

Hinson's was a run-down little building—a country store selling mostly milk, bread, soda pop, snacking foods, beer, wine, cigarettes, and fuel. Asphalt sheet siding covered its outer walls to hide the rotting boards. Two gas pumps sat out front where Paw filled up his truck, while Daddy carried two of Paw's ice chests into the store.

"Carrie Jane . . . Dylan . . . you two go inside and get yourselves a Coca-Cola and a pack of nabs and have Billy Ray put them into one of those ice chests. You'll need them later on when you get hungry and thirsty," Paw told us.

With bare feet and clad only in a blue with white piping one-piece swimsuit, I opened the store's weather-worn wooden screen door to go inside. The fading image of a brownie—on the door's rusting screen—tempted me with its chocolaty-tasting drink. The pungent odor of stale cigarette smoke hung in the air. Its wooden floor suffered from dry rot, leaving gapping areas between the boards and exposing the ground below. I stepped gingerly across the room towards the drink coolers, trying to avoid getting any splinters into the soles of my feet. Dylan rushed past me, as if unaware of the store's deteriorating conditions; he was smart enough to keep his shoes on.

"And just what in the hell do you two little shits think you're doing in here?" Daddy looked up from where he had squatted, packing the chests with ice and beer.

"Paw told us to come inside . . . to . . . get a Coca-Cola and a pack of nabs," Dylan hesitantly replied. He must have thought Daddy was going to reach out and strike him, taking several steps back into me.

"Ow! You stepped on my toes," I hollered, hopping about on my one good foot, while trying to console the other with my hands.

Dylan pretended not to hear me.

"My goodness, Billy Ray, those two kids of yours sure are growin' up fast," we heard a man's voice from behind us. "And if that Carrie Jane ain't gettin' to be a right purty little thang."

"Aw right, Miss Priss, where are your manners? You tell Mr. Hinson *thank you*," Daddy said as he lifted a filled ice chest and headed for the counter, bumping one side of it into me.

I stumbled forward, picking up a splinter in my other foot along the journey.

"*Ow!* Uh . . . thank . . . you . . ."

Daddy cut his eyes in my direction and flared his nostrils, as a non-verbal warning of what would happen next if I did not show proper respect to my elders.

". . . Mr. Hinson."

"'. . . *gettin' to be a right purty little thang,*' " I thought to myself. "Just what's that supposed to mean?"

Wayne Hinson sat behind the counter upon a high stool—elevated above his customers like a self-important man—sucking on cigars all day. When he smiled, his round, fat face pushed against his eyes, causing them to squint into beady dark dots. The black hair on his head always looked greasy from using what I thought had to be an entire tube of Brylcreem. His purple tinted lips were varnished with saliva, after licking them every time he took the soggy-ended cigar from his mouth. Behind him, on the wall, hung pictures of scantily dressed women he had taken from the pages of magazines and calendars. Mama refused to do business at his store, calling him "*a dirty ole man,*" but

Daddy said that Wayne was "*nothin' but a misunderstood good ole boy,*" known for selling beer on Sunday mornings, violating the state's blue laws.

"Wayne, would you hand me a couple packs of Winston?" Daddy asked.

He rang them up on the cash register along with the ice and beer, and Dylan and my treats.

"Billy Ray, I see your kids are wearing their bathing suits. You and Raymond thinkin' on taking them swimmin'?" Wayne blew cigar smoke down into my face, staring at me while talking to Daddy. It stung, causing my eyes to blink.

"Reckon so. Daddy said it was about time they learnt a few things," my daddy replied, then shrugged his shoulders in disinterest and went back to collect the second ice chest.

Paw walked inside the store and took two more sodas from the drink cooler and forced them into the first ice chest.

"It is going to be hot out there today, children," Paw said. "I believe you are going to need more to drink than that." As he paid the bill, it occurred to me that Paw had never been so generous, but I wasn't about to ask him for a candy bar.

"Don't you kids go out there and get yerselves drowned, now—*ya hear?*"

Wayne started heaving up this deep, guttural racket that was stored within the walls of fat inside his abdomen. By the time it rumbled through his stomach and out of his mouth, it sounded more like a plump woman's *tee hee-hee.* I wanted to stick my tongue out at him, but Paw said it was time to go.

***

We rode several miles from Hinson's Store headed towards Deep River, where Freemans Mill—originally an old gristmill—once operated on its banks from the 1800s until 1944, passing ownership through various hands during that time. About one hundred feet from the river's edge we turned down a wide dirt driveway, passing a spacious two-story home, with colonial-styled columns supporting its rocking-chair front porch—a mansion by area standards. The property belonged to a Mr. Thomas Carlyle Jennings, said to be a self-educated, well-to-do man, who moved there during the early 1930s and took ownership of Freemans Mill, converting it into a repair shop. That was where Paw acquired his welding, electrical, and mechanical skills. Because of Mr. Jennings, Paw became the first Brine male in our line to learn a trade outside of farming or making moonshine.

The truck stopped in front of a metal gate where Daddy exited the truck and unlatched it, and Paw drove us through, without a word ever passing between them—as if they had made this same journey together many times before.

The elongated, egg-shaped pond rested in the valley of a pasture. Cattle grazed along its bank, but the herd headed for the surrounding woods as we drove up. I could barely contain my excitement for wanting to jump up-and-down and shout out how happy I felt for being picked to do something—*anything*—but thought Daddy might get upset with me.

I remained still.

"Now, don't you young'uns get any stupid ideas like trying to pet those cows—especially you, Carrie Jane, 'cause sometimes you ain't got the gawddamn sense God gave a goat. Those cows will trample your sorry little asses," Daddy warned us. "And if there is anything left of y'all, I'll finish that off with my belt—*y'all hear me*? Oh . . . and you might want to watch where the hell you step, 'cause your Paw won't be lettin' you back in his new truck with shit all over ya."

After backing the boat into the water, Daddy and Paw stripped down to their swimming trunks and started in on the contents of an ice chest, leaving Dylan and me to play by the shoreline.

The water covered over twenty acres of land—an earthen tub scooped out by man and machine. It did not flow into any tributaries or other bodies of water, but sat stagnant like an oversized cesspool. Bugs lit upon its stillness, creating faint ripples. As I stepped ankle deep into the dismal liquid, I could not see my feet. It did not seem wise to venture far into the murky waters. Dylan stayed close by.

It seemed like a few hours passed before Paw and Daddy finished their first ice chest of beer. Emptied brown-colored beer bottles littered the ground, awaking a sense of displaced color to the green and black and white and grey landscape. As the early afternoon sun began to heat up, Paw grew restless.

"Come on, young'uns—let's take this here boat out for a ride on that thar lake."

Paw (generally) paid close attention to his diction, carefully choosing his words and accent. I thought his manner of speech made him appear a little bit smarter than most people we knew, by avoiding our hard-sounding country dialect. Though he never achieved a public education beyond the sixth grade, he was well read in all manner of science and mechanical publications and novels. He often corrected my own poor speech performance, but never Daddy or Uncle Johnny's. When I asked him why, he told me they were *"too old to correct their bad habits."*

But it was after consuming too many beers that Paw began to sound like the locals and became reckless in his behavior.

Daddy remained on land, saying: *"Somebody's gotta watch these beers, else the gawddamn cows 'll be drinkin' 'em."*

After Paw hoisted Dylan and me over the side of the boat and onto the deck, he climbed aboard and began yanking at the outboard motor's pull cord. It sputtered, as if out of breath. Then stopped.

"Shit," he muttered.

He yanked a second time, only for it to let out a cough. Then stopped.

"Son-ov-a-bitch!" he hollered.

On the third try, it cranked.

"About gawddamn time," he swore.

As the boat floated upon the water, Paw moved forward towards the pilot's chair; he swayed to-and-fro like a drunken sailor, uncertain which order to place his feet upon the deck. He sat down hard onto the chair, causing the boat to rock erratically from side-to-side, and causing Dylan and me to stagger.

"Come 'ere, young'un," Paw slurred, pulling me upon his lap. "I'm gonna let ya steer."

And so, my maiden voyage was underway. Seated at the helm, I clutched the large black wheel with my small awkward hands, trying to maintain control over the fifteen-foot aluminum watercraft—with its faded red stripe around the hull and silver-grey wetted surface area. The boat crept ahead, creating soft wavelets in the water. A light breeze stirred by its movement gave us a brief cooling sensation from the pond, disturbing the heat momentarily. Only the loud *blub-blub-blub* sounding off the 30hp Evinrude engine made it difficult to hear anything else around us.

Dylan sat next to us—portside—with his arms crossed and bottom lip protruding into a pout; he never liked being second. He scrunched up his face at me, so I stuck my tongue out at him. Sometimes, Dylan and I never needed to exchange words. But Paw always chose me first over him. He said it was the proper thing to do—a *ladies first* sort of thing.

"When you was born," Daddy told me, "your Paw was takin' trash out back to dump into the burn can, and when I hollered out the backdoor '*it's a girl,*' he got so excited, he came running inside the house still holding onto that damned trash."

I had been his only granddaughter for five years until Dinah came to live with us, but that didn't seem to change things. Dylan being the oldest grandson was important according to Paw, but being the oldest granddaughter was special. He purchased me a fishing rod for my fifth birthday, though I had never used it. He tied both ends of a twisted nylon rope to a tree branch in his front yard and notched the ends of a board to make me a seat for a tree swing. He even *played house* with me once, allowing me to serve him dirt pies. These grandfatherly kindnesses he did while sober and *during* his leisure moments. I learned early in life there were two times to never encounter Paw: while at work or when drunk.

A sudden gust of wind flipped my long dark hair into Paw's barrel-shaped chest and clipped him in the face.

"*Young'un, you need to get that mess cut,*" I thought I heard Paw shout over the engine's noise.

Another time he shifted my weight from one knee to the other.

"*Young'un, yer cuttin' off my circulation,*" I thought I heard him bellow . . . or was that thunder?

Paw was afflicted with a terrible case of varicose veins.

The boat propelled us methodically through the water as we inched our way around the pond. Paw helped me turn the wheel as we rounded the curved bank and headed back to where we began. Then suddenly—without warning—he took hold of the throttle and accelerated the motor. *"Brrrrrrr"* the outboard roared. Zigzagging waves replaced the ripples, as water splashed over the bow onto the foredeck . . . or was that rain?

"Paw, make it stop!" I screamed.

I thought I heard him laugh . . . or was that the wind?

As the shore grew closer my heart raced from fear; I could no longer control this runaway vessel. So, I aimed it straight ahead, searching for any port to drop anchor in the midst of our drunken storm. At least I would be able to make us stop at the water's edge. A voice suddenly came to me that faded in and out of the stirred waters and from the motorboat's dying engine, after Paw pushed the kill switch. It told me that it was not such a good idea to drive a watercraft on dry land.

"What in the hell are ya doing, young'un? Don't you know any damn better than to try such a stupid thing? You tryin' to get us kilt?" Paw's slurred reprimand seemed kinder than those given by Daddy, though the words did not make me feel any better.

"I should've let Dylan drive the boat instead of you. He wouldn't have pulled such a damn dumb stunt!"

Then another voice echoed off shore.

"Carrie Jane, ya stupid little shit! Somebody needs to kick your scrawny ass just for being a fuckin' dumb ass! God only knows why I was given such a boneheaded child!"

I looked for the voice, and saw Daddy staggering over to the shoreline.

Perhaps Daddy and Paw were right: I was a stupid child and made a terrible helmsman. But I wanted to ask Paw why he made the boat go so fast, when I had never driven one before. I wanted to tell him it scared me, but I couldn't. I remembered what Daddy told us of how Paw would get drunk and beat Uncle Johnny and him every Saturday when they were growing up, just in case they had done something wrong during the week Paw did not know about. He beat them with anything he could get his hands onto. Daddy said some of the beatings were so bad, Uncle Johnny and he were unable to sit and barely able to walk for days.

"When I got big enough, I wasn't about to let my daddy beat on me any-gawddamn-more, so come Saturday morning I'd ride my bike out into the woods behind the house and hide. Johnny could never run fast enough, and always ended up getting an ass whuppin'," my daddy said. "I didn't come back until Daddy had passed out on the couch from drinking too many beers or bottles of liquor. By Sunday morning, he'd sobered up and forgotten whatever-in-the-hell it was that had pissed him off."

It was a Saturday. I remained still.

"No more boat drivin' fer you today, young'un," Paw announced.

Before restarting the outboard, he lifted me off of his lap and had me trade chairs with Dylan. My brother looked a sickly shade of green as he took his place behind the wheel, though Paw did most of the steering. After a few more passes—*slow* passes—around the pond, Paw edged the boat closer to shore and told us to go back to playing. I stood knee-deep in water watching as Daddy and he walked back to the comfort of a shade tree to begin drinking their second ice chest of beer. They laughed and cursed, and I could hear my name. It stung.

As the evening sun began to ebb its way towards the horizon, Paw rose to his feet and tottered as he moved towards us, like one unaccustomed to walking on dry land.

"Since you're no good at drivin' a boat, I reckon it's time I learnt ya how to swim, Carrie Jane."

Paw lifted me up, and I found myself heading for deeper waters, riding in the arms of a delirious leviathan. He stopped at what felt like the center of the pond. The waters came up to Paw's chest, so I grabbed onto his neck and held fast, fearing I would sink to the bottom if he dropped me. My frantic movement caused him to step backwards, and we sank deeper inside the waters. As the stagnant liquid rushed up to my head, I dug my feet into his stomach in an attempt to climb onto his shoulders.

"Whoa, calm down there, young'un; we just stepped into a little hole." The strong odor of alcohol emitted from his lips as he spoke.

"Now, com'on, young'un, and let go. You're gonna learn to swim, 'cause I'm gonna learn ya—just like I once showed Billy Ray when he was about your age."

His words triggered the memory of a story Daddy once told. Something about Paw got drunk one Saturday and took Daddy and Uncle Johnny to Deep River, where he tied four fruit jars to Daddy—one attached to each arm and leg—and tossed him into the river; only one of the glass jars broke and Daddy nearly drowned.

"No . . . no, I don't wanna learn, Paw!"

I struggled to retain the grasp I had around his neck, but Paw was too strong for the grip of a five year old. I could hear Daddy's laughter from the shore.

"Don't be such a gawddamn little chicken shit," Daddy berated me. "Go ahead and let your Paw learn ya how to swim."

Paw laid me face down onto the water's surface.

"I gotcha," he assured me. "Don't worry . . . I gotcha."

Only I did not believe him, arching my head towards Heaven to keep my face out of the water.

"You're never gonna learn to swim with your head raised up like that."

Holding my body down using one arm, Paw placed his free hand on the back of my head and pushed my face underneath the water.

This would be my other *shit hole*, only this time, who was my boogeyman? I fought to get free of Paw's hold, but water filled my nose and mouth as I attempted to breathe. I could hear the dull splashing my arms made as they struck the water around me. I could feel my feet kicking against Paw's fleshy abdomen. Water filled my ears, and a great pressure seemed to be smashing in the sides of my head. It was like being placed inside a tomb of water, as it molded around my body to take me under so we would be one. The life-sustaining and life-taking substance had taken control over my body. My eyelids fluttered rapidly, while strobes of darkening light passed from me. My breathing stopped, and the struggle left me. I had given in without a choice. This was how it felt to die; I was drowning. Where was my mother? She knew how to save me, like before, from the ditch.

Then something abruptly lifted me out of the water. Was it the hand of God? Was I going to meet Jesus? I felt a blow from behind and then another, like a hammering sensation between my shoulder blades. I could not see anything. The only noise I could hear was this shrill ringing inside my head. Water sprayed forth from my nose and mouth. I choked, unable to catch my breath. Another blow struck me from behind. Short, raspy wheezes allowed me to suck in a little air.

"Aw, she'll be alright," I heard someone laugh from a great distance.

The laughter grew louder in my ears, as specks of light filtered through my eyes.

"*Carrie Jane, yer nothin' but a gawddamn baby—afraid of a little water!*"

That was not the voice of Jesus I heard; it was Daddy.

Paw carried me back to dry land and rejoined Daddy. After regaining my breath, I sat down and sobbed.

"After I've finished this beer, it'll be your turn, Dylan. Maybe I'll have better luck with you than with that sister of yourn."

Though Paw snickered, his voice sounded agitated, as if displeased with the day's events.

Dylan stood silent by the pond's edge. A look of certain doom descended upon his face, as one whose fate was determined by roaring-drunk giants and well-oiled sea monsters. He could not escape them without divine Providence on his side. As Paw tossed the last empty beer bottle to the ground and clumsily gathered himself to his feet like a legless giant, a noise rumbled from behind us. Rolling up the dirt driveway from which we earlier came, salvation appeared in a green Plymouth station wagon.

"What in the hell do y'all want?" Daddy shouted.

"Billy Ray, it's getting late and I think it's time for Dylan and Carrie Jane to come home," Mama said after stepping outside of the car, holding Dinah in her arms.

"Well, Daddy's gettin' ready to learn Dylan how to swim."

"Never mind," Paw said, while half-sitting and half-falling back onto the ground. "This has been nothin' but a waste of my damn time and money."

"Then do whatever in the hell you like," Daddy snapped at Mama. "Yer goin' to, any gawddamn way."

She loaded us into the backseat, and Grammy drove away.

"Did you two enjoy your day at the pond?" Grammy asked, while looking at us through her rear-view mirror.

"I don't like being first," I answered, bursting into tears.

We never went back to Jennings Pond, and I never learned to drive a boat nor how to swim.

I never wanted to.

CHAPTER 8

A Lazy, Crazy Interlude

Grammy possessed two flaws in her character that kept her from being the best grandmother a child could ever want: She was always *lazy*, and sometimes *crazy*.

For as long as anyone could remember, Grammy never cleaned her house. And she hardly ever cooked a meal, unless it was one of those thirty-plus minute frozen *TV* dinners, which consisted of an aluminum plate sectioned-off into areas that held shriveled pellets impersonating peas-and-carrots, freezer-burn tasting whipped potatoes, a near peach-*less* cobbler, and some chewy meat-*ish* product—a forbidden meal in my mother's house, but my secret childhood comfort food that gave my life a feeling of order.

When Paw came home looking for something to eat, he settled for one of those *TV* dinners, chow-chow relish, potted meat, souse meat (*head cheese*), pickled pigs' feet, or some other strange jarred concoction he kept on the kitchen table of various animal parts that looked like something from a lab experiment gone awry.

When I turned six, Grammy showed me how to boil pots of water to cook macaroni and cheese from a box and packaged hot dogs; how to use an electric can opener and heat-up canned peas; and how to set the oven at 425 degrees for *TV* dinners, all while standing on a kitchen chair in front of her stove. Afterwards, she would have me drag the chair over to the kitchen sink where I would wash the dishes.

Mama was none too pleased to learn I had become the *chief cook and dish washer* when staying at Paw and Grammy's house, but Daddy shrugged it off as if those were the duties every six year old performed.

"Hell, so what if Carrie Jane learns how to cook at her age? Good-gawd, Irene, what do you expect the young'un to eat when she's staying there? It's sure-as-shittin' Momma ain't getting off that lazy ass of hers to cook anything."

"Well, it's not safe for her to stand on a chair over a stove with pots of boiling water on hot burners, while your mother sits in a chair smoking cigarettes and watching the television," Mama complained.

Daddy rolled his eyes at her, as if she did not fully grasp the situation.

"From the first grade on, Johnny and I went to school on damn empty stomachs, because Momma wasn't getting out of bed to help us get ready. When she wasn't sleeping, she would be laid up in the bed eatin' chocolate and readin' those Grace Livingston Hill novels. And if Johnny and I wanted to eat, *we* stood on chairs and cooked at the gawddamn stove when we were younger than Carrie Jane.

"Shit, I'd rather the young'un eat her own cookin' than Momma's any day of the gawddamn week. The few damn times I can ever recall her cookin', Momma fixed a large pot of white potatoes that lasted over a week. She'd leave the gawddamn things sitting in the pot on the stove until they had *by-gawd* turned blue, and my daddy kept eating that shit until he finished them off, because my daddy doesn't believe in throwing anything out. How in the hell he never got sick is still a mystery. Johnny and I figure he must have a gawddamn cast-iron stomach."

"And you don't have a problem if Carrie Jane washes your mother's dishes?"

"*Oh, hell no!* Somebody has to. At least Momma hasn't *went off* on her like she used to do with Johnny and me," Daddy said, then shook his head and scoffed, as if halfway talking to himself while remembering.

"Momma . . . Momma would say: '*Billy Ray . . . Johnny, now you two had better warsh those dishes in the sink.*'

"Then she'd just fly off the handle for no good reason and throw the clean dishes we had just warshed out the backdoor, telling us they weren't clean enough, and how we had to re-warsh them in dirt. And for the broken ones—" he paused as if caught in the past, his countenance turning grey, "as for the broken ones, she told us we had better figure out how to put them back together or else she'd whup us.

"We'd be bawling our eyes out saying: *'But Momma, these here dishes won't go back together.'* Then she'd get out the belt and beat us, and when Daddy came home, she'd tell him that *we* broke the dishes, and he would beat us all over again.

"Johnny and I were just two little boys sittin' in the dirt, trying to put together some gawddamn pieces of broken glass."

For a moment, Daddy grew silent on the matter.

"Come to think of it," he smirked, "what's the gawddamn difference in you having her iron clothes, or Momma letting her at the cook stove? She'll most likely end up burned from one gawddamn thing or the other."

Mama walked away.

Grammy spent most of her days in a faded green recliner that remained upright; propped her dirty bare feet on top of an ottoman; watched television game shows all morning, soap operas during the afternoon and late-night programs into the early morning hours until the three networks went off the air; consumed bags of chocolate candy bars and bottles of Coca-Cola, or a diet soda called *Tab* (formulated for those with a unique palate) that only she could drink; smoked cartons of cigarettes; and took pills from several medicine bottles for her thyroid, phlebitis, nerves, and various other nondescript ailments. The smell of urine reeked from around her recliner, as there were times Grammy would not get up to walk to the bathroom. Some nights she even slept there, because she just didn't feel like hoisting herself out of the recliner, walking to her bedroom, and climbing onto the twin bed that stood next to Paw's bed—where she slept with her upper body raised to an approximate seventy-degree angle by an enormous piece of foam wedged between her box springs and mattress. Over the years, Grammy found herself unable to lie flat while sleeping, as it cut off her breathing and caused any undigested food matter to return during the night, making her choke in her sleep.

When at home, Grammy lived in her pajamas. She kept the top rolled and knotted in fashion underneath her fifty-two triple-D unsupported bosom, leaving her ample mid-section exposed. Since she rarely washed her clothing, one could reasonably conclude she seldom took a bath with soap and water. Instead, she bathed in piles of cigarette ashes from her overflowing ashtrays that spilled off the top of a credenza standing next to her recliner. Some of the ashes dusted the unopened and unanswered stacks of mail she kept on the credenza's surface. Still more ashes covered the linoleum flooring of the den, whose color had long since lost its original luster and turned to that of a grainy soot pattern. Only Grammy lived among her ashes every day, appearing to be unaffected by their presence, or even those smoldering coals that fell off the ends of her lit cigarette into her lap. She had become oblivious to the pain or just too lazy to brush the hot ashes away.

During the days I stayed at their house, Grammy received maid service, where I served her drinks and meals on top of a *TV* dinner tray. Before long, she had me sweeping the floors, dusting the furniture, changing the sheets on the beds, and taking the wash out to hang on the line.

Trying to reach the clothesline proved the most difficult task for me to perform. Grammy became agitated and even angry with me over the couple of times I told her I couldn't do it, which meant she had to get out of her chair to help me.

"If you can't handle a simple chore around here, I'll just take you home right this minute."

I knew that Grammy meant what she said, and that just wouldn't do, because Paw and Grammy's was the only place I could escape to from my own home. My solution was to improvise and not bother Grammy with any more problems. Luckily, the clothespin bag hung heavily on the line, so I discovered if I pulled on the bottom of the bag until I could stand on it—stretching the clothesline wire downward—I could reach the center. That meant the wet sheets drug the ground, which meant that Paw became agitated to discover he had to frequently rewire the sagging line.

When Daddy heard that I had acquired the job of pinning his parents' wet clothing to the line, he told us how he applied his own brand of mischief to the task during his boyhood days.

"I once took a pair of Momma's bloomers and put a clothespin on one end, then stretched them as far as I could on the clothesline until the elastic in the waistband snapped, and then pinned them on the other end to dry. They were already big enough to fit a gawddamn cow," he chuckled. "The beating she gave me afterwards was well worth it to be able to watch those big ole baggy bloomers fall down around her ankles."

I never tempted fate by tampering with Grammy's oversized undergarments. They were difficult enough to hang on the line as it was. Instead, I found pleasure in burning the trash.

The first time Grammy handed me a matchbook and told me to take the household garbage out to their fifty-five-gallon drum used as a burn can and set it on fire, I was excited and a little scared. For starters, I wasn't tall enough to safely reach over the top of the can to drop the trash inside, and I had never lit a match. I found a cinder block I managed to drag inch-by-inch across the yard and place next to the can, giving me just enough height to push the grocery bag of garbage over the can's rim. Sometimes the paper sack proved too heavy for me to lift, and it toppled over—littering the ground with tin cans, glass bottles, and everyday household refuse, scattered among the bits of oxidized metal flakes that had fallen off the burn can—leaving me to pick up each piece of trash by hand and toss it over the rim of the drum.

At first, I wasted several matches attempting to get one lit. From fear of burning myself, I would release the match into the can while scraping it against the striking surface on the matchbook cover. When I did get one struck, I'd singe my fingers from holding on to it for too long as I tried to light the grocery bag. Sometimes I left the cover open with the match heads exposed, resulting in the phosphorus tips all igniting at once, creating a flash fire in my hand. I immediately dropped it into the drum. But after much practice, I taught myself how to strike a proper match and start a sizeable blaze. It didn't take long for me to realize that finer bits of paper took flight, performing a fiery aerial display, only to have the twirling bits of light and sparks descend upon the ground. If it landed on dried grass and debris, I chased after the small fires, stomping them out with my little girl shoes. It seemed wiser to burn the trash in the early morning, while the dew was still wet on the grass.

I thought best not to tell anyone that Grammy let me burn the trash, because even I knew it wasn't something a six year old should have been doing. But then one day, while admiring the flames whip above the can's opening, Paw walked up behind me.

"What are you doing out here, Carrie Jane?"

"Um . . . *Burning trash?*"

"Who said that you could burn the trash?"

"Um . . . *Grammy did?*"

"You wait right here until I get back. And don't go anywhere near that burn can!"

A few moments later Paw returned from inside the house. His face shown beet red and his teeth appeared to be set on edge, as if he had been drinking vinegar. While the tone of his voice sounded angry, it wasn't me he was angry with.

"Carrie Jane, don't let me catch you out here playing in fire, again. Do you hear me?"

"Yes'ir."

"And if your grandmother should ever tell you to burn the trash without *first* asking my permission, don't do it. Do you hear me?"

"Yes'ir."

"Now, you get back to the house, while I take care of this mess."

"Yes'ir."

Grammy refused to look or speak to me for some time. She puffed on her cigarette, flicking the ashes against a filled ashtray in an agitated manner.

"Humph!" Grammy finally snorted. "Your Paw's done jumped all over me. He says he had better not catch me letting you burn the trash until you're older. He says I need to get off of my fat, lazy butt and go do it myself. Humph!"

In a few short years—when I was tall enough to look over the top of the burn can—Grammy handed me another book of matches to resume my previous chore.

"Here! It's about time you started burning the trash, again," she informed me. "And I done told your Paw. After all, you are getting paid to help out around here."

Even at the age of six, I wondered if I should be receiving some sort of compensation for my services, after I had overheard Mama tell Daddy that if I was going to clean their house, I should not be expected to do it for free. Grammy said she couldn't afford to pay me, so I decided to take up the matter with Paw.

"Paw?" I took in a deep breath and blurted out the next question: *"Do I get money to clean your house?"*

"I guess so," he huffed.

So, when each stay came to an end, and I had to return home, I asked him for my pay.

"Here," he said, shoving a dollar or two towards me that he took from his billfold, as if I had taken the last money he had to his name.

Now, over the years Grammy kept parakeets. As one died off, she replaced it with another. She rarely fed or supplied fresh water to the poor little things, so their life expectancy proved short lived. And she never-ever cleaned the cage they lived inside. When I came to visit—despite what my age was at the time—she always ordered me to do the feeding and watering, as well as the cleaning of the defecated, urinated mess left behind. The one time I failed to take care of her pet, Grammy let me know.

"My bird died," she telephoned to tell me two days after my last visit, "and it's your fault. You didn't feed or water it like I told you to. Next time your Paw gives you a couple of dollars for cleaning the house, you need to give the money to me to pay for my bird you killed."

So, the next time Paw gave me two dollars, I handed it over to Grammy. She slipped the bills into a side pocket of the oversized brown leather handbag she kept next to her recliner without saying a word. It was a lesson learned that when hired to do a job, I had best complete the work, else not get paid. And I, also, bore the eternal guilt and responsibility for having neglected one of God's smallest creatures.

***

It wasn't all work, though. Grammy played board games. She taught me how to play Parcheesi, Chinese Checkers, straight checkers, Scrabble, and even card games like Rummy, Solitaire, and Rook. Sometimes she showed me how to paint-by-numbers or crochet with yarn, though I never got past the chain stitch.

Then there was Grammy's obsession with *televangelism.*

It seemed like those *Ministers of the Gospel* flooded the television airways during my childhood, many whose names have long since been forgotten. Some promised that salvation and blessings and riches would come your way if you financially supported their ministries, with a small, tax-deductible donation of ten dollars or more.

When I asked Daddy if he had ten dollars to spare, so we could be saved, blessed, and wealthy, he said, *"I reckon we're shit outta luck, 'cause I ain't sendin' my hard-earned money to some man preachin' through a gawddamn television. If I wanna get preached at, I'll spend ten dollars on beer, then stay home and listen to your momma."*

As for the times I watched religious broadcasts with Grammy, they ultimately created more questions than answers for a small child.

"Grammy, how come that *TV* preacher named a church after himself and not Jesus?" I asked.

"Because that is what he said Jesus told him to do. Besides, Jesus doesn't need to have a building named after Him, because He chose that preacher as His messenger to spread His Word," Grammy reasoned.

"But Grammy, if *TV* preachers can heal sick people, how come they ain't healing those old people in the hospital?"

Grammy pondered for a moment before giving me an answer.

"Preachers need money, so they can continue talking about Jesus on the television. And since they won't let you keep any money whilst staying in the hospital, if the sick people are ever able to leave and go home, they can mail their money and prayer requests directly to these preachers, and then they'll be healed."

"So, how come Jesus never asked for money? He was poor."

"Humph!" she snorted. "He didn't have to. He was the Son of God. And they didn't have television back then."

Now, there was this one *TV* preacher, who offered Grammy a holy light switch cover made of paper. In a mass-produced form letter, he vowed to fly over her house—in his holy airplane at approximately one a.m. on a certain date—and bless her dwelling through the power of that light switch cover. She had to act fast and send him a small, tax-deductible donation of ten dollars or more, or risk losing this special one-time blessing. Grammy posted a check that same day.

You would have thought Jesus Christ, Himself, had given her a signed, limited-edition, self-portrait as she attached that paper cover—with the *TV* preacher man's name and image printed on the surface—onto the light switch over her recliner.

"Bless me, Lord Jesus, and bless me, preacher man," Grammy shouted whenever she looked at her ten-dollar holy relic, held in place by transparent tape.

On the night of his plane's promised arrival, she had me sit up with her to wait for this special anointing.

Now, when one lives in the stillness of the country nights—when the only sounds you can hear are the crickets and bullfrogs singing in the darkness, and the moon and stars emit the only light you have to navigate the nighttime sky—one acquires a keen sense of hearing and night vision. So, several minutes before one a.m., Grammy actually arose from her chair, and we stood together watching from the front porch and listening for that *TV* preacher's airplane to fly by overhead. By 1:15, though, there was no sign of the preacher or his plane, so we went back inside.

"He must have been flying so high up there with the Lord," Grammy reasoned aloud, "we just couldn't see him."

Convinced she had received her blessing, Grammy continued to send him and others like him money for holy thermometers guaranteed to keep the true believer's house comfortable in any type of weather; blessed bottles of colored water to splash on yourself should the Devil tempt you into spending money on material possessions; holy brochures and books claimed to be written by God, Himself, (only through some *TV* preacher man's pen); and anything else their devoted followers—like my grandmother—were willing to buy with a small, tax-deductible donation of ten dollars or more.

***

For as long as he lived, not a dime of William Raymond Murphy Brine's money went to support these televangelists or their ministries—Paw had no time for religion. Grammy sent them money she earned from peddling merchandise. She sold Knapp Shoes to the local farmers, Amway detergent, and various Blair products ranging from knickknacks to food flavorings. Cosmetics were her specialty, holding the position of a

Beauty Counselor for both Vanda and Studio Girl cosmetic lines. On the days she managed to get out of her recliner—get bathed and dressed—Grammy traveled throughout Guilford, Randolph, Davidson, Forsyth and surrounding counties, delivering orders and taking new ones from her mostly female clientele.

Probably from the time I was potty-trained and could chew my own food, Grammy would take me with her to peddle merchandise. It was through Grammy that I became acquainted with the world around me. While most of her customers were just plain country women, who lived on farms, there were a few ladies she visited that resided within the city limits of Greensboro, High Point, and Winston-Salem (or just plain *Winston* as the locals called it). While the city folk were nice to Grammy and me, many tried to put on airs like they were smarter than us country types, sometimes joking about how we killed our own chickens and hogs and grew most of our own food, while they—being more civilized—bought theirs at a grocery store.

"Grammy, how come those ladies think we don't go to the grocery store? Next time, I'll tell 'em my mama buys her chicken at the Winn-Dixie!"

"Carrie Jane, sometimes it's best to be polite and keep that bit of information to yourself—if you want to make another sell," as Grammy so aptly schooled me in her trade wisdom.

I figured they were just suffering from living on this tiny bit of land not big enough to keep a goat entertained and from being surrounded by too much concrete and asphalt. Though I had never seen a sidewalk or paved driveway until Grammy took me to the city, I did find they were much easier to walk upon than the dirt, mud holes, and gravel surfaces we called *driveways*.

There were, yet, two other differences between the country and city women that fascinated me: it was in what they spent their money on, and the way they paid for their purchases. The *citified* women—dressed in their polyester clothes and costume jewelry—always bought the most merchandise from Grammy. Their money supply seemed endless, buying up trinkets and doodads to sit around their houses, or bags of make-up they would never wear, or items to fill their daughters' hope chests. And these ladies rarely gave Grammy cash money, as most of them paid by check. If they ever used cash, they had nothing less than a crisp twenty-dollar bill, while the country women's money looked like their clothing: old, faded, and made of cotton. I often wondered how long some of the country women had kept those folded dollar bills hidden inside of their worn change purses, just so they could buy themselves a tube of hand cream or a bottle of vanilla flavoring.

When I was six years old, Grammy took me to a house that sat in the poor section of Greensboro, where no one had paved driveways or concrete sidewalks. Except for the city limits sign, you would have thought you were still in the country, because no one had bothered to patch the road's potholes.

Now, this particular house, which had once been painted white, had turned a weather-beaten shade of grey and sat upon brick columns that looked as if they would collapse from years of structural pressure and erosion. A wide porch stretched across the front, lacking any sign of ever having railing. The front yard was one large patch of swept dirt, with a few scattered tall trees serving as shade.

Grammy pulled her car over to the side of the house, but instead of getting out, she turned to me to speak. Her voice rattled—not her smoker's rattle, where it sounded like loose, rusty nails were piercing her vocal chords. It sounded more like a small clot of blood had left her heart on a foolish mission and became trapped in her larynx, nervously bouncing within a confined space while trying to determine if this had been a wise decision.

"Carrie Jane . . . I need you to listen really good. Now, uh, I never brung you to a house like this before, because you were too young. But since you are nearly old enough to start school, I'm hoping you'll be able to understand. The lady who lives here—Mrs. Jackson—is my friend and has been for several years." Grammy paused to clear her throat, and then lowered her voice to almost a whisper. "And she's a colored lady."

She held her breath for a second as if expecting some type of response, but I sat still, not knowing exactly what to say.

"I want you to go in with me and be polite to Mrs. Jackson. And don't you say or do anything that might offend her."

Separating people by the color of their skin seemed a confusing concept, especially to a child. There were all manner of animals, birds, and insects in the world, whose colors spanned every hue on a color wheel, but I never heard anyone say they hated a brown kitten because it was brown or a yellow kitten because it was yellow—or they hated a white lamb because it was white or a black lamb because it was black. It wasn't that way with people; most judged you by how light or dark you looked on the outside, as if anyone was given a choice. Grammy said God decided that.

From Grammy's younger photos, you could tell her skin tone had once been dark—*darker than mine*—but over the years it had acquired a yellowish-brown tint from too many cigarettes and staying mostly indoors. Sometimes she had her blackish-grey hair cut short, and a beautician would perm and paint it light or reddish brown, or she simply wore wigs. Though it seemed she tried to hide who she was from those outside the family, you could still see the Cherokee heritage in her broad nose, full round face, and high cheekbones.

"And you have to promise me one thing," she continued. "You cannot tell your Paw, your daddy, or your momma about this. You understand?"

"Yes, ma'am."

"Lord only knows what might happen to your poor Grammy if anyone ever found out I had taken you into a colored woman's house."

We were greeted at the front door by Mrs. Jackson— a smiling, large-framed older lady, dressed in a brightly colored flower-patterned smock, who kept her thick black-and-grey hair pulled back into a bun, with short, curly stragglers forming delicate little ringlets against her unblemished dark skin.

Inside her home hung pictures on the walls of babies, children, adults, and old people. All were black. On one wall, there hung a picture of Jesus. He, too, was black. In the homes of white people, I noticed their Jesus was white, which led me to wonder *what color was Jesus?* When I later asked Grammy, she said no one seemed to know for certain, and it didn't really matter.

As I sat there on Mrs. Jackson's spotless red velvet couch (with the plastic slipcovers), while Grammy and she discussed the latest line of cosmetics, I had this feeling someone was watching us. Turning around on the couch, I noticed a dozen small dark faces pressed against the living room windowpanes and the front door screen, looking from the outside in. They soon started pushing and fussing with one another, each jockeying for a better viewing position.

"Don't you shove me like that," one child said.

"Then get outta my way, dog meat," said another.

"I'll knock you out for calling me that!" shouted the first child.

"Just you try it, dog breath!" yelled the other.

Their fighting was no different than the encounters Dylan and I shared. And Mrs. Jackson proved to be no different from Mama.

"Y'all children had best behave, or else I'll tell William when he gets home. Don't y'all go embarrassing me in front of my company."

Mrs. Jackson had walked to the front door and stood with her hands placed firmly on her billowy hips. The children scattered from sight.

"Dear Jesus," she exclaimed, rubbing her hands together as she walked back towards her chair, "I just don't understand what gets into children these days. Do you, Mrs. Brine?"

Before Grammy could answer, I broke the Brine family code of silence Daddy had imposed upon me: *"Children are to be seen and not heard, unless they want a gawddamn belt acrost their backside!"*

"Mrs. Jackson, are all them yer young'uns?"

I heard Grammy's oversized false teeth click together as her upper plate fell on top of her lower. She tried to speak; only her teeth were now blocking her tongue. As Grammy fumbled with her dentures, Mrs. Jackson answered me as if I had always been part of their conversation.

"Lawd no, child!" Mrs. Jackson laughed heartily, slapping her thighs with the palms of her hands as she rocked forward in her chair. "My husband William and I only have two children, and they're both grown, married, and have children of their own. These here are just neighborhood children, whose momma or daddy's busy working or can't be found, so we just look after them like they was ours. Why, all God's children need to be loved. Don't matter if it's by their real parents or someone else. Isn't that right, Mrs. Brine?"

Grammy readjusted her false teeth and returned them to their original position. Seeing how I had not offended her friend and customer, Grammy gave up one of her rare smiles.

"You are right, Mrs. Jackson; you are surely right."

***

Mental illness varies in degrees as to how it affects each of its victims. Some express it through rage or acts of violence; some wonder about aimlessly as if lost or confused; others ramble on of paranoid delusions or of hearing voices; while some sink into a major depression; or simply lose the will to live. What causes one's grey matter to misfire could be anything from heredity, illness, poor dietary choices, head injuries, substance abuse, life's overwhelming experiences, and even evil entities of the human and spiritual realm.

No one seemed to know exactly what drove Grammy's bouts of insanity. Her bizarre antics nearly pushed those around her over the edge. Even Paw's own spirit suffered from her affliction.

"If you were a drunk, at least I'd know what to do for you," he once raised his voice at her in frustration. "*But this?* I can't do a damned thing to help you!"

And no one seemed to know exactly what to do for her, either, though no adult seemed particularly interested in hearing what she might have to say. On her melancholy days, when her mind could rationally reflect, Grammy told me stories about her childhood— stories that not even her own sons had ever heard. While I was nothing more than a small child and could not comprehend everything she said at the time, I tried my best to sit still and listen . . . and remember. Seated in her den on the faded green recliner, dressed in the same unwashed pajamas, her mind retraced a time and tales she could not forget. Perhaps it was her way of trying to purge her soul of childhood demons.

"My great-great granddaddy was a Cherokee Indian chief and my great-grand momma was a Cherokee Indian princess from my momma's side of the family," Grammy began. "My people came from Lumpkin County, Georgia, but my parents moved to Atlanta where my siblings and I were born. My poppa—Ezra Smith—he was a white man.

"Oh, did I ever mention Poppa was a second cousin to President Abraham Lincoln through Lincoln's grandmother, Bathsheba Herring? He was, indeed!

"Well, anyway, Poppa died back in 1918 from the Spanish Flu when I was just four years old. My momma, Lessie, she moved us—Ruby, my older brother Wesley, and me—to High Point, so she could get a job in one of the hosiery mills. That's where she married the meanest man who ever drew a breath—Silas Simpson— but we called him *Ole Man Simpson.* He was already living from pillar to post and wouldn't keep a job. It seems like we moved every other month just so he didn't have to pay the rent. Momma kept working in the mills and handing over her pay to him at the end of the week, and lord only knows how he spent it all. He drank most of it away, I suppose, and then he would come home and beat us all with a razor strap—even Momma.

"I remember how Momma once asked him for a nickel to buy a pair of shoelaces, and he told her to go find some string and make her own. Why, we couldn't eat our supper until Ole Man Simpson ate his fill first. If we had chicken, he would gnaw the meat down to the bone, leaving Momma to feed us a broth she made from boiling the bone in a pot of water.

"Then this one time all we had to eat was oatmeal for supper. He threw a fit and pitched it—pot and all— behind the *johnny house*. He said he didn't like the taste of the stuff, so nobody in his house was going to eat it, either. Then he got gone for a week, so we figured the best way to get rid of him for a while was to cook up a pot of oatmeal. It worked every time."

Grammy cackled at how they outwitted their adversary. Then taking a drag from her cigarette and a sip from her bottle of soda pop, she continued on with her story.

"We'd heard of how Ole Man Simpson's first wife had lost her mind. Before she died, he would charge money for people to come and see what a crazy woman looked like. They said folks came from miles around in their buggies and horseless carriages to line up at his front door. After she died, he decided to put an ad in the newspaper to sell their eight children. Some came out of curiosity just to see if the ad was real, but there were no takers. He said he reckoned he had to keep the sorry things. After having a daddy like that, who would have thunk that all four of his boys grew up to become preachers? Before Ole Man Simpson died, though, he had a stroke and lost his own mind. They had to strap him down to his bed, because he kept screaming about all of the demons he swore were running around in his room."

Grammy's mind drifted; her story took a different path.

"I . . . I don't know whatever became of my baby sister. I tried to find her," her voice softened to almost a whisper. "She was just a baby when they took her away."

"But Grammy, I thought Aunt Ruby was your older sister?"

"No, not Ruby—*Nessie Mary Simpson*. Momma had a child with Ole Man Simpson when I was eight years old. A few months after Nessie Mary was born, Ole Man Simpson took off and never came back, and even left his own eight children behind. And Momma, she was sick at the time; she had *Heart Dropsy*. Her legs would fill up with fluid and then burst.

"Momma would say: '*You see these?*'" Grammy's voice cracked as she tried to choke back her tears.

"'You see . . . you see these large veins in my chest, Pansy? They are going to take me away someday.'

"Momma . . . Momma died when I was fourteen."

Grammy sat sobbing for several moments, dabbing her eyes with tissue from a box she kept on her upholstered ottoman. I remained silent until she stopped.

"Who took Nessie Mary?" I asked, afraid that Ole Man Simpson might have stolen her.

"Well, after Ole Man Simpson finally left us for good, Momma could no longer take care of the baby or the rest of us children for that matter. She asked his oldest daughter, Maggie, if she'd temporarily take the baby to raise, just until Momma got to feeling better. Maggie was sixteen and unmarried at the time, and she said no one would believe the child was her half-sister, and she would have a hard time ever finding a husband or being accepted by the locals. So, Momma packed up Ruby, Wesley, Nessie Mary, and me, and we took the train to Raleigh to live with her mother, Mary Catherine. Ruby, Wesley and I called her *Grand Momma*. Now, you talk about a mean woman . . ."

Grammy paused in the middle of her sentence taking another draw from her cigarette, while carelessly dropping ashes onto her exposed rounded belly.

"Um, let me see . . . right up until Poppa died, we all lived with Grand Momma at this boarding house she ran in Atlanta. She didn't come with us to High Point, but moved to Raleigh with her second husband,

Stephen Smith, to open up a general store. We called him *Granddaddy Stephen*, but he was actually Poppa's uncle; he was a kind old man, who wanted to take all of us in after Ole Man Simpson ran off. But not Grand Momma; she said she'd feed just some of us, only if Momma wanted us to stay there, she had to give up the baby. Grand Momma had her other daughter— Momma's youngest sister, Aunt Selma—hand Nessie Mary over to the folks at the orphanage when they came to pick her up. Momma . . . *Momma just couldn't do it.*"

This time the tears streamed down Grammy's face before she could reach for another tissue. She wiped her eyes with the sleeve of her pajama top.

"Poor Momma just cried and cried, but Grand Momma told her to stop that nonsense, because she wasn't ever going to get her baby back. I once tried to contact the orphanage in 1939, but they refused to help me find her. They said she was too young to be bothered . . ."

"Was your grammy an Indian, too?" I interrupted.

"*Mary Catherine?* Oh, yes . . . yes, Grand Momma was a dark-skinned woman with raven black hair. She never learned how to read or write, but she could sure count money. Not long after we moved to Raleigh, she had me working behind the store counter, taking money from customers. It was the first time I'd ever seen a two-dollar bill; only I made this man change for a twenty. When Grand Momma realized what I had done, she went running out the door and tackled him in the middle of the street. She then straddled that man and beat the tar out of him until he gave her every last penny he had in his pockets."

"Did she beat you up, too, Grammy?"

"No, not that time. But once—when I wasn't quite twelve years old—Grand Momma asked me if I knew how you got pregnant? I pointed to a nightgown of hers that she had hanging up to dry and answered innocently, *'By wearing that?'*

"Why, she slapped me so hard acrost the face, I flipped over the back of a chair. After that—for some reason—she decided that I couldn't come out when there was company. She'd lock me away in my bedroom and say: *'Now you go get under your bed and crack rat turds!'*

"But then Grand Momma was mean like that to every one of us—especially to Ruby, after she married that *no 'count* Chester Lowman and had their first child. They couldn't afford the milk to feed the baby. Granddaddy Stephen brought them milk from the store; only Grand Momma went over to where they were staying and took it back. She said the baby would have to starve until Ruby or Chester came up with the money to pay for it."

Grammy grew silent for several seconds, as if in deep thought.

"God says it's a sin to hate another person, but I can honestly say that I've never despised a person as much as I do that Chester Lowman," she said, her voice rising to an agitated state. "He's hardly ever worked a day in

174 | COLIN HARDIMAN

his life, and if not for Ruby, their children would have starved to death. At Christmas time, he pretended to collect money for the Salvation Army and hid the donations underneath his house inside mason jars. Then he bought this nasty liquor people called *rotgut* and mixed it with Paregoric. It sent him into these blind rages where he'd beat poor Ruby so badly that she wound up losing all of her teeth.

"And I'll tell you what he did to me . . ."

As Grammy paused in mid-sentence, the corners of her mouth turned downwards and her nostrils flared with each breath.

"I'll tell you what that horrible man did to me one time," she snorted. "When I was fourteen years old, right after Momma died, I went to stay with Ruby and Chester. They'd moved from Raleigh to High Point— years before they settled over yonder in Davidson County. Ruby worked second shift at a hosiery mill there in town, and I worked first shift at the same mill. At the end of every week both Chester and Ruby made me turn over my entire paycheck for room-and-board, and I even had to take care of their three children while Ruby worked, clean their house, and put supper on the table by five o'clock.

"One evening, I was so tired after working in the mill, I laid down to take a nap. Sometime later I heard Chester screaming: *'Why's my supper not on the table?'*

"I jumped out of bed and ran into the kitchen. *'I'm sorry. I fell asleep, but I'll get it fixed right now,'* I tried to tell him.

"'That's no excuse; you're supposed to have my food on that table at five o'clock!'

"He removed his belt, wrapped the leather around his hand, and started beating me with the belt buckle. I ran into my bedroom and locked the door, but he kicked it in and chased me around the room, striking me over and over again with that buckle. The next thing I remembered was waking up on the floor, lying there in my own blood. Chester had put a large gash into the side of my head. So, I bandaged it up the best I could, cooked supper, and then ran away to live with a neighbor for a few months, until I married your Paw."

Grammy's eyes appeared to lose focus and she stared off into a great void, as if watching a film replay in her mind.

"But what happened to Mary Catherine?" I interrupted her.

"Oh, yes, Grand Momma, well . . ." Leaning towards me, Grammy lowered her voice to a half whisper, as if afraid someone might overhear her. "Now, you have to promise me that you won't go off and tell your Paw, your daddy, or your momma."

"I promise."

"Good, because they wouldn't like it one bit if they knew I told you this. A couple of years after I married your Paw, Granddaddy Stephen died, so Grand Momma sold the general store and moved to High Point to live with Ruby and Chester. Then Grand Momma took sick. While she lay dying on her bed, she started screaming and hollering something fierce about how she could see Momma, reaching down to her from Heaven.

"Grand Momma shouts: *'I can't reach you, daughter, come closer! It's because I'm a sinner I can't reach you. Lessie says for me to burn my playing cards . . . somebody burn my playing cards right now, in this-here room!'*

"My brother Wesley found a metal waste can, and Ruby set those cards to blazing with a match and lighter fluid.

"Then Grand Momma sets to wailing something awful: *'Lessie, I still can't reach you! Come closer, daughter; come closer before it's too late for me! The Devil's coming to pull me down to Hades for what I done to you! It's not enough . . . Lessie says to burn everything I own, even my clothes and shoes!'*

"So, we burned everything she owned—right there in the room—and just like that, she died. A few seconds later, all of the windows burst wide open. Paper and anything not nailed down blew all over that house like we was having a tornado. We swore Momma must have grabbed hold of Grand Momma's hand and took her spirit away, just right before the Devil came looking for her."

Now, telling such a story to a small child might not have been the wisest thing for her to do, but it wasn't Grammy's tales that scared the bejeezus out of me at the age of six—it was Grammy's sister, the *not-so-*Great-Aunt Ruby.

***

During that spring of 1966, Grammy stopped selling her merchandise and almost-never left the house. On the days I stayed with her, she talked with Ruby on the telephone, or Ruby drove from Thomasville—over *yonder* in Davidson County—to visit with Grammy when Paw was out working on a welding job, gone on a fishing trip, or to a stock car race. This posed a problem for Grammy, seeing that her sister was warned to stay away after Paw's $4,000 went missing.

"Carrie Jane, you have to promise me something," Grammy ordered me, more like a command than a request. "You cannot tell your Paw *or* your daddy *or* your momma about this."

"Yes, ma'am."

"Lord only knows what they would do to your poor Grammy should they ever find out Ruby's been here."

It was during her visits with Grammy that strange things were said—frightening things that a child, let alone an adult, should never become familiar with. It was through Great-Aunt Ruby that I first heard about the dead man buried under Paw and Grammy's house. It was from Aunt Ruby that I first heard about superstitious beliefs and evil spirits. While Ruby never deliberately intended for me to hear talk of such things, my being there presented her with a financial dilemma.

"Carrie Jane, you take this-here dime and go off and play somewhere in the house, whilst I talk with Pansy."

Now, I had never been one to just wander off and mind my own business—not even after being bribed with a dime. Once I walked out of their sight, I crawled around the corner on my hands and knees—slightly poking my head into the den where Grammy and Ruby couldn't see me—to hear what was being said.

"Have you gotten all them silver dimes like that fortuneteller told ya to get, Pansy?" Ruby asked, with her voice lowered to an audible whisper.

"Yes, and I've stacked them over the top of every doorframe in the house just like she said," Grammy replied.

"That's good. I didn't think I could feel those evil spirits like last time when I's here. Remember, she said for you to buy more silver just in case there ain't enough in those dimes to protect ya."

The next week, Grammy's china cabinet became filled with silver items of every sort: silverware, serving platters, teapots, utensils, and candlesticks. Afterwards, she confined herself within the house, refusing to even take Mama to the grocery store, because Ruby warned her that something evil lurked outside ready to snatch her soul away. Grammy took to wearing a low-crown white cap adorned with metallic red, silver, and gold moons-and-stars. Ruby claimed it possessed special powers that would keep evil spirits away from her.

Then Ruby told Grammy not to go back into her own bathroom, because something *bad* lived in there (and it wasn't the dead man buried in the ground underneath the middle bedroom, as he only haunted the basement, or so according to Ruby.) No, this evil spirit would snatch Grammy down into the toilet if she dared use it. Some fortuneteller (*again*, according to Ruby) insisted Grammy purchase a specially *blessed* trashcan, which the evil spirits of the world could not penetrate.

"You'd best be givin' me $100, just like you did for that thar hat, so I can go pay for yer trashcan," Ruby told her.

It wasn't like Grammy frequented the bathroom much, but she completely stopped using her toilet after that. The *$100* trashcan became her personal port-a-john.

I even became afraid to use Grammy's bathroom, afraid some unseen force would pull me down into the bowl. Having spent time in the boogeyman's ditch, I didn't want to take a chance on living inside another cesspool, unable to escape. Unlike Mama, it seemed doubtful Grammy could or would try to pull me out. While not an easy feat, I held the contents of my bladder until I returned home that evening.

Then one morning, while Paw was out on a welding job, Ruby came calling with a most terrifying message:

"*Pansy,*" she whispered, "*I done heard from that fortuneteller the Devil is on his way here to your house. So, you'd best git over to that graveyard at Mills Methodist Church come nightfall. She says he won't be able to find ya there, with it being sacred and all. But I'm gonna need some money to pay her. She cain't make any promises, but she says she might be able to stop him.*"

Grammy opened her purse and handed Ruby all of the paper money she had inside.

"Pansy, if you ain't heard back from me 'fore dark, remember, you need to skedaddle to that graveyard, else you got trouble comin' yer way."

And I was terrified.

Then about noon—shortly after Ruby had left—Paw returned. I got up the nerve and made tracks for his garage. Nearly out of breath and about to wet my pants, I ran through the garage's opened doorway and up to Paw, who was standing over a lathe, reshaping a piece of broken metal. I grabbed onto the legs of his work pants, pinching his flesh between the material and my fingertips.

"*Ouch!* What in the hell . . ." Paw let out a sharp scream and leapt backwards out of my grasp. "Gawddamnit, child, what is your problem?"

"*Paw . . . Paw,*" I gasped, "*I gotta go . . . I gotta go home.*"

"What? Go home? Can you not see that I am busy?"

"*But I've gotta go home right now, Paw. Please take me home . . . or can I stay with you?*"

"Carrie Jane, you cannot stay here with me. You are only six years old, and a girl at that. Your mother would throw a hissy fit. Besides, tell me why you have to go home so damned bad?"

"*I ain't . . . I ain't feelin' so good.*"

"Then tell your grandmother to take you home. I have work to do."

I stood there for several seconds staring at Paw, waiting for him to change his mind. If he would not take me, how would I get home? I could not ask Grammy. I had just left her in one of those staring trances she had recently acquired, while sitting perfectly silent in her recliner and looking off into what appeared to be a void of nothingness. She would remain like that for several hours. That meant Grammy was too incapacitated to drive. And since Mama didn't have a car to come and get me, if I attempted to walk the mile-and-a-half journey home by myself, Daddy would have given me a well-deserved beating.

"I said for you to go back to the house. Now, *go on!*"

Paw stomped a booted foot at me as if he was shooing away some stray dog. And like a stray dog, I ran back to their house.

As the sun slipped down into the horizon, no telephone call came from Ruby. Paw found me seated outside his front door on the top step. I dared not reenter their house—afraid the Devil might sneak up when I wasn't looking. And if Grammy decided to head off towards the cemetery, it was certain I wouldn't be following her. The thought of ditches, boogeymen, devils, evil spirits, and graveyards caused my pint-sized body to shudder from a fear brought on by the words of adults.

"Carrie Jane, why are you sitting out here?"

"I gotta go home, Paw."

"Why didn't you ask your grandmother to take you home?"

"She cain't."

"Why in the hell *'cain't'* she?" Paw angrily mocked.

"She ain't feelin' too good."

"She is *not* feeling well!" Paw huffed, correcting my poor speech habits. "Well then—go on—get inside the gawddamn truck before I change my mind."

Not another word passed between us, until he turned his truck around in our yard and told me to get out.

"You had better not ever pull another stunt like this one. Don't waste my time with your nonsense. You either come with the intent to stay, or do not come at all. Is that understood?"

"Yes'ir."

"It is pronounced *yes sir*, Carrie Jane—not *'yes'ir'*."

"Yes . . . sir," I mumbled.

As much as I wanted to tell Paw what had been said that morning, I was too afraid: afraid he would not believe me, and afraid the Devil might change his mind on who to visit. So, as the evening turned to night, and I was told to go to bed, I did something I had never done before: I cried out for Daddy.

"Daddy, Daddy, help," I screamed from my bed. *"The boogeyman is after me!"*

"The boogeyman?" Daddy laughed as he entered my bedroom. "Why in the *hell* would you think the boogeyman is after you? You know good-and-damn-well he lives in that gawddamn ditch acrost the road."

"Nuh-uh, not . . . not since Aunt Ruby let him out."

"What the fu . . ." Daddy said, scratching behind one of his ears in an agitated motion. "Has my momma been lettin' that old gummy bitch come over while you're there?"

Breaking my oath to Grammy, I nervously nodded my head up and down and asked something I had never asked before and would never ask again:

"Daddy . . . can I sleep in your bed tonight, so the boogeyman won't get me?"

For a moment, he stared at me as if I had just made the strangest request he had ever heard.

"Sleep in my bed . . . oh, why the hell not. I'd be afraid, too, if I'd seen that gawddamn Ruby today. I've stepped in better lookin' piles of dog shit than that ugly, crazy-ass bitch!" Daddy released a fake shiver and contorted his face as if even the thought of Ruby frightened him.

He had no more laid me down on his side of the bed and left the room when—literally—all hell broke loose.

"Billy Ray, why are you letting that child sleep in our bed? I don't care what she's afraid of. She has her own bed to sleep in."

Mama's fuss with Daddy became interrupted by my screams, after their white bedroom curtains reflected off moonlight into what I believed to be a ghostly image. And then the telephone rang, with Paw on the other end of the line telling Daddy to get over to his house right away, because Grammy had mentally and physically "gone off her gawddamn rocker."

As soon as Daddy drove away to encounter Grammy and her demon, Mama stormed into their bedroom to exorcise mine.

"Young lady, you are going to stop this foolishness and get out of my bed right this instant! I don't care one iota what you're afraid of, but you can be afraid of it in your own bed."

Sliding out of their bed and trembling onto the soles of my feet, I returned to my own covers without uttering a word. It seemed in my best interest not to challenge Mama on the matter. Just before dawn, I found myself startled from sleep by the sound of Daddy returning home.

"What a gawddamn crock of shit, and I'll be a son-ov-a-bitch! I don't know if Momma is faking it, or if she is flat out fuckin' nuts?" Daddy's voice rose upon every word he spoke, each syllable shook as if rolling from thunder.

"Billy Ray, have a seat so you can calm down. I'll go in the kitchen and fry you some bacon and eggs, and fix a pot of black coffee," Mama said.

"I don't want any *gawd--damn* food! The last fuckin' thing I want to do right now is eat."

"Okay, Billy Ray . . . then tell me what happened." Mama's voice lowered as if it might influence him to lower his own.

"You're not gonna believe this shit, Irene!" Daddy continued to elevate the conversation. "I've seen my momma pull some crazy-ass stunts, *but nothin' like this!* She had Daddy, Johnny, and me chasing her all over *gawddamn* High Point last night. Before that, she had us running her down in the cemetery over at Mills Methodist Church, tripping over headstones and trampling graves in the dark. This story is about the biggest pile of steamin' horse shit I've ever smelled . . . and it's because of that *gawd--damn* Ruby . . . if I could get my hands on her this minute, I would strangle that fat fuckin' sausage neck of hers down to the size of a wiener! She'd never be able to swallow as much as a *gawd--damn* pea for the rest of her *gawd--damn* life!"

"*Billy Ray?*"

"'*Billy Ray*' nothin'! That damnable woman's been filling Momma's head full of shit and trying to drive her crazy for years. I reckon she finally damn-well succeeded! My daddy said last night if that gawddamn woman ever steps foot back inside his house, he'll blow her fuckin' brains out and claim self-defense."

"You don't think he meant . . ."

"*I'll be damned if he didn't!*"

"What . . . *what* did Ruby do to her?" Mama's voice sounded anxious for the story to continue.

"*Well,* I no more drive up in their yard when I see Momma running out the side door—*in nothing but her damn pajamas*—with Daddy on her heels. Then Johnny drives up, so the three of us start chasing after her towards the cemetery next door. Any woman who can move that gawddamn fast should be able to get off her lazy ass and clean her house." Daddy huffed out a half-chuckle, but soon raised his voice, again, in agitation.

"We corner her around this headstone and tell her she needs to get on back up to the house, but she starts carrying on about how that *gawd--damn* Ruby told her the Devil was going to pay her a visit last night, along with this bullshit about some fuckin' fortuneteller saying she had to be on consecrated ground for protection. Except for the moonlight, we cain't see a gawddamn thing. After tripping and stumbling over everything dead and alive, we manage to grab onto her, and the three of us have to literally drag her fat ass back up to the house, with her kicking, and clawing, and screaming that she's not goin' in there, not as long as the Devil's inside.

"'*Wee--ll,*' I says to her, '*I reckon we'll find him sittin' at the kitchen table, suckin' on one of your tasty Tabs and eating one of those delicious frozen dinners you're always buying, 'cause there ain't much else in that house for him to help himself to.*'

"So, we sit her down on a chair in the den, and now she won't say a word. Instead, she starts writing us these gawddamn silly-ass notes.

"'*I'm having a heart attack,*' she keeps writin' over and over again.

"Daddy says: '*How in the hell do you know you're having a heart attack?*'

"Momma writes back a note that reads: '*I just am . . . take me to the hospital.*'

"She gets into the car, and the four of us head for High Point Memorial Hospital. The emergency room nurses lay Momma out on this gurney, and she has yet to speak a damn word to anybody.

"The emergency room doctor takes one look at her and says: '*This woman's not having a heart attack; she's suffering from anxiety!*'

"Momma sits upright on that gurney, rips open the front of her pajama top exposing her big old, naked breasts, and screams out at that doctor: '*Cain't you see I'm having a heart attack?*'

"I've never been more embarrassed in my entire, *gawd--damn* life. If she had not been my momma, I would have knocked her ass onto that floor."

"For goodness sake, Billy Ray!" Mama's *shame-on-you-for-saying-such-a-thing* voice echoed into my bedroom.

"By gawd I would have! And I ain't a damn bit sorry for saying it, either. I think Daddy feels the same way. He's so embarrassed at the hospital, he just walks out of the room, while Johnny, he just stands there with his mouth hanging open—speechless.

"So, I finally say: '*Momma, pull your top together; you're goin' back home.*'

"'*I'm not going back there,*' she starts hollering.

"'*By gawd, I'll drag you back to that car if I have to,*' I say to her.

"Then that damn, no-good-for-nothin' doctor butts in with his bullshit: '*You cannot lay a hand on her.*'

"'*Watch me!*' I tell him.

"So, that son-ov-a-bitch says: *'If you touch her, I'll tell my staff to call the police and have you arrested. This woman doesn't—legally—have to go anywhere with you.'*

"Momma ties her pajama top into that stupid looking gawddamn knot under her breasts, walks out of the hospital, down the sidewalk, and into the street. And she just keeps walking. We follow her in the car, but she refuses to get inside.

"Daddy says: *'I've had about all of this shit I'm willing to put up with.'*

"I stop the car in the middle of Elm *by-gawd* Street, and the three of us have to literally drag her fat ass back inside the car, with her kicking, and clawing, and screaming. We get back to the house, but Momma stays outside, while Daddy calls that Dr. Lou Gundy over in Archdale—*right in the middle of the fuckin' night*—and asks for help gettin' commitment papers on Momma."

"So where is your mother right now?" Mama asked.

"She's on her way to Butner," Daddy replied.

***

During World War II, the United States Army opened Camp Butner—named after Surry County native, Major General Henry Wolfe Butner. They used the grounds for military training, an army hospital, and a stockade. After the camp closed in 1947, the State of North Carolina purchased 13,000 acres of the 40,000-acre campsite (along with its hospital) from the United

States government for one dollar and established a facility for treating the mentally ill. Just north of Raleigh, John Umstead Hospital sat in the unincorporated town limits of Butner, North Carolina—an area Daddy came to describe as *"out in the middle of gawddamn nowhere."*

Most folks just called it *Butner.*

Paw and Daddy traded off every other Sunday as to who would be the one obliged to visit Grammy. Each complained when his Sunday came around, as both said they did not want to be bothered. They had other pressing matters to attend to: Daddy had beer to drink, while Paw had fish to catch or a stock car race to watch . . . *and* beer to drink. Paw traveled to Butner alone, except for the few times Uncle Johnny joined him. Aunt Roberta remained at home. As for Daddy, he always brought Mama and us children along for the visit. Daddy said that was because the doctors wanted Grammy to be around family, as it might speed up her recovery process. That meant we purchased a bucket of Kentucky Fried Chicken on the way, so we could have a picnic at a park on the hospital grounds.

During the early weeks after her committal, we saw little of Grammy. Daddy would go inside the hospital for twenty minutes or less, only to return to say she had suffered a *"bad spell"* and would not be coming outside to join us for *KFC* in the park.

That *bad spell*, as Daddy called it, had something to do with Grammy's failure to cooperate with the hospital staff and follow hospital rules, like when she refused to take her medicine. Or the times she broke into a running, screaming fit, banging on doors and windows in an attempt to escape her locked ward. When the orderlies finally caught up with her and were able to strap her down to a gurney, they placed a block inside her mouth—so she would not bite off her tongue—and then proceeded to give her electroshock therapy.

When Grammy finally *behaved* and was allowed to join us in the park, she was unrecognizable. Seated on a picnic bench, she barely moved (except for her continuous shaking hands). Her eyes appeared fixed inside her head like glass marbles, as if no memory, no thought, nor recollection of life existed behind them. Her skin had turned ashen, as if almost unto death. Her hair appeared dry and frayed and brushed haphazardly about her head. Her once long fingernails were broken down to the quick. Her speech sounded slurred, and her sentences fractured and incomplete.

"Y'all fine—here to take me home," she often uttered in a low voice.

Our grandmother had become zombie-like.

***

During one Sunday afternoon visit to Butner, there were no empty parking spaces near the front of the hospital, so Daddy drove to a different area of the facility we had never been before.

"Billy Ray, I'm not sure we should be in here," Mama said to Daddy. "It looks like someone might have forgotten to lock the gate."

"I'll park wherever I gawddamn-well please," Daddy growled at her.

A high-security, chain-link fence surrounded what appeared to be a parking area behind the hospital to house service vehicles. As Daddy parked the automobile, I spotted a man dressed in a hospital-issue robe, nightgown and slippers wandering freely about the confined space, stopping at every vehicle for a brief look inside before moving on to the next.

"I'll be back as soon as I find out what the hell my momma's been up to this week," Daddy complained. "I gotta feelin' I've wasted another gawddamn Sunday with this bullshit!"

Daddy's agitation lingered as he got out of the vehicle and slammed the driver's door shut with such force the window rattled and the car shook. As he stomped off towards the hospital, Daddy failed to notice the lone figure, who had redirected his course and was headed in our direction. But Mama did. She leaned across the front seat and locked the driver's side door. When she locked her own door, I realized my mother was afraid. Then the man veered off behind a panel van parked on the other side of us, as if he had changed his mind. Mama let out a brief sigh, only to suddenly gasp for air.

A short man, with disheveled brown hair, stood staring at my mother through the passenger side window of our two-door, navy-blue, 1965 Ford Galaxie that Daddy traded his truck for (*a purchase Mama said we couldn't afford*). This man possessed the strangest blank stare on his face, as if hypnotized, unable to willfully control any rational thought or movement. Reaching silently into a robe pocket, he pulled out a penny, which he carefully dropped through a small opening at the top of the car window next to where Mama was seated; she had forgotten to roll her window all of the way up.

Except for the fidgeting Dinah seated upon her lap, Mama sat perfectly still looking straight ahead, unable or unwilling to turn her head into the stranger's direction. The man continued pulling out one penny at a time and slipping it between the glass and window seal. Each copper coin slid down the inside of the glass and bounced off of the door's padded vinyl interior onto the floorboard or onto Mama's lap. It was as if we were seated inside a vending machine, and the door would magically pop open so the peculiar man could collect his purchase once enough pennies were deposited inside.

Up until that point, Dylan and I had not uttered a sound from the backseat, but something was about to break that silence. And that *something* would be me. Now, there always seemed to be a quality lacking in my character. Perhaps it was good old-fashioned commonsense, or my inability to keep quiet (even in a potentially dangerous situation) that got me into so much trouble. Daddy had recently taken to calling me *"motor mouth,"* along with his favorite profane adjective to give it that certain *oomph.*

"You gawddamn motor mouth—you shut the hell up right this fuckin' minute, or else I'll slap you so gawddamn hard your head will spin!"

In this case, I had never seen anyone—except for Ruby—who just gave away money, without first having to work for it. If she would give me a coin to leave the room, why wouldn't this insanely generous man give me money for the asking? Not long before, a man had handed me free sticks of gum at the hospital in High Point. Now, at the age of six, I supposed that strangers gave little children gum and money just because they wanted to.

"Mama, Mama, Mama, ask him if he has any dollar bills!"

"Hush," she hissed at me in a whisper, still looking straight ahead.

Only I wouldn't let the matter end there.

"Hey, mister, do you have any dollar bills?"

Mama's head snapped over her left shoulder towards me. *"I told you to shut up!"* she hissed louder, but with a tremble in her voice. Her eyes opened wide with a look of fright about them, as if something had terrified her to the core—something close to Grammy's Devil and the boogeyman.

After a few minutes, the flow of pennies ceased, and the short man simply turned and walked away without ever speaking a word to us. Mama had something to say to me, though.

"Carrie Jane, what were you trying to do? Get us all killed?"

"But he didn't do nothin' 'cept give us some money," I replied.

"Young lady, sometimes you don't have the first ounce of sense. You know better than to speak to strangers. And you sure don't know what someone might try to do to you in *this* place. Next time someone walks up to the car, you *keep* your mouth shut, you hear me?"

"Yes, ma'am."

Dylan, who had remained quiet, leaned over and whispered in my ear: "*Stupid.*"

Of course, I stuck my tongue out at him, and then called him a "*doo-doo head,*" just before he punched me in the right arm.

It all proved most confusing for me; perhaps I was too young to grasp the ways of adults. You could take chewing gum from an elderly, infirm white man at a hospital, and you were expected to say, "*Thank you,*" even though you were warned *not* to take candy from strangers and *not* to talk to strangers, but you couldn't return a wave from a neighborly, elderly black man outside a doctor's office, nor could you speak to a peculiar-acting short man wearing a *johnny gown*, giving away free money in the parking lot of a mental hospital. And I couldn't be afraid of my boogeyman (at least not in my parents' bed), but Mama could be afraid of hers.

***

Over the next several years, Grammy would frequent John Umstead Hospital, sometimes receiving more electroshock treatments during her stays. Her mental behavior ranged from momentary sanity to a complete breakdown of mind and body. Most of her illness centered on the Devil, but sometimes on Jesus. One morning, she claimed Jesus stood at the foot of her bed, saying she needed to be baptized to wash away her sins. Whether real or a vivid dream, Grammy hurried out the side door and headed for the birdbath standing in front of their house—even ripping open her pajama top in what some might have described as a maniacal episode. Leaning over the concrete basin, she splashed its contents onto her partially exposed body, until Paw, Daddy, and Uncle Johnny chased her across the yard—like fullbacks trying to intercept their renegade wide receiver running in the wrong direction—while vehicles swerved about Highway 62, as drivers attempted to catch a glimpse of this religious sporting event.

There were even times Paw and Daddy told us children to try and talk Grammy back into her house, after she claimed the Devil had returned. We often found our poor grandmother hiding out in a nearby field sitting on cinder blocks or curled up on the ground behind her car. Only nothing could convince her to go back inside—not even the threat of returning to Butner.

After that day, when Ruby declared the Devil was coming to pay Grammy a visit, I became secretly convinced that something unnatural, yet, unseen lived within Paw and Grammy's house—some noxious entity left there by Ruby. My childlike, impressionable mind imagined it roamed through their rooms at night, in search of Grammy or another victim. Though it would be a few months after her breakdown before I could return to my grandparents' home, on those nights I did, I fell asleep with my eyes opened—while waiting for the dawn.

CHAPTER 9

The Codes

When I was growing up, both Daddy and Mama lived by their own set of parental codes. Daddy's possessed a lyrical tone, along with a bit of dramatic rhetoric, like when he hollered at my brother Dylan or me:

"Gawddamn you little sorry-ass-piece-ov-shit, you either do as I say, or I'll kick your fuckin' ass so hard your nose will bleed!"

While Mama never held a command over the English language quite like Daddy, she always got her point across. She would simply say to us:

"Just you wait until your daddy gets home, and then you'll be sorry for the way you've treated me."

While both differed slightly in content, their codes narrowly translated in my six-year-old mind to mean:

I would always do what Daddy said or else; I would never upset Mama or else.

The *or else* wasn't always a belt to the backside and sometimes remained to be seen, or in its most simplistic form—*experienced.*

My life to that point had been confined to the idiosyncrasies of my immediate family, Daddy's beer-drinking buddies, Grammy's customers, and a few of the locals who frequented Paw's garage. The only child I socially interacted with (on a regular basis) was Dylan. I didn't have to be polite to him; he was family. That meant my social skills needed improvement, and my manners were unpolished at best.

Then there was my baby sister, Dinah. Knowing nothing about the evolution of babies, I watched over a series of months as she grew in size; went from Mama's lap to a high chair; and the weaning of her from a bottle to being spoon-fed strained baby food from a jar. She began teething, learning how to crawl, then walk, and finally attempting the English language. Once Dinah mastered the art of walking, though, my nonexistent role as *big sister* took a different direction: She suddenly became *my* responsibility, as Mama needed someone to serve as Dinah's charge while she went about her daily housekeeping chores. Being a boy, Dylan was never assigned to baby watch. Mama said that boys did not do *"girls' work."* Only my shortcomings as a babysitter soon rekindled Mama's bitter resentment towards me.

"Carrie Jane, watch your baby sister while I fix supper!"

A declaration of war would be declared if I did not obey Mama's command.

Though our house was small, it proved a difficult task in trying to keep up with Dinah. Our only interior door was for the bathroom, granting her complete access to every bedroom, the living room, kitchen, and hallway. I had to chase her from room-to-room to keep her out of trouble. The only person who seemed to get in trouble, though, was me. Dinah discovered early in life how to get her way. If I tried pulling her away from something she wasn't supposed to be doing, she would let out one of her blood-curdling screams, causing Mama to come running to her howling baby's rescue.

"What are you trying to do . . . *hurt* my baby? Don't you pull on her little arms like that! You'll tear them right out of their sockets."

"But Mama, Dinah was playing in Daddy's ashtray, so I tried to . . ."

"I told you to watch your baby sister. You're supposed to be making sure she doesn't get into anything. You've made me stop what I was doing, and now I have to wash up her little face and hands. This is your entire fault, Carrie Jane. Next time she does something like this, I'll take a switch to you.

"And another thing, if my baby grows up and acts like you," Mama hissed at me, "it will be *your* entire fault!"

According to Mama, all of Dinah's sins—past, present, and future—rested upon my shoulders. I did not like being a big sister.

Then without fail, Mama *always* ended her tirade against me on a particular note:

"I hope that someday when you have children of your own, they treat you as badly as you treat me. I hope they act just like you!"

You wouldn't call her remarks a blessing. But at that moment, I felt like a miserable failure as a big sister and even worse as a daughter. Things would not improve for me.

Dinah, though, would soon become the least of my worries. A different challenge awaited me: the first grade. Before I was able to enter those hallowed doors leading to higher learning, Daddy placed certain *pre*-school expectations upon me. For starters, he told me that if I knew what was good for me (like not having my backside drop kicked about the living room floor), I had better make all *A's*, like those Dylan achieved in the first grade.

And then there were the *teensy* problems with my thumb and hair.

***

"What are ya? Some kinda gawddamn baby who sucks on her thumb all of the time? No young'un of mine is gonna start school with a thumb in her mouth. You'll take that damn thing out of your mouth or else lose it," Daddy warned me. "And you'll get that fuckin' rat's nest hair of yers cut, or else I'll take out my gawddamn pocketknife and do it myself."

My thumb's invisibility powers were waning, because Daddy could see me. While his threat gave me cause for concern, it was Mama's words that touched upon my vanity.

"Carrie Jane, if you don't quit sucking your thumb, when those baby teeth fall out and your permanent ones come through, you will have buckteeth."

"What's *bucket teeth*?" I asked her.

"Buckteeth . . . not *bucket teeth*. It is when your upper teeth stick out of your mouth instead of staying inside."

That almost frightened me enough to stop, until Dylan started making fun of me. *"Bucky,"* he nicknamed me, following me around the house making smacking noises with his mouth, while protruding his upper teeth over his bottom lip like he was imitating a beaver.

"Hey, Bucky—*smack, smack, smack, smack, smack*—you'll soon be able to eat your corn off the cob through a picket fence."

"Oh yeah, pig face, I'll give you the cob, so you can gnaw on it outta your trough."

"Will not!"

"Will, too!"

"Will not!"

Thump! Dylan used his fists between my shoulder blades to prove I didn't know what I was talking about. I balled my right hand into a fist and punched him in the arm—then ran.

Despite all of the threats made, name-calling, flying fists, and the possibility of looking like a dam-building rodent, I continued to cradle the thumb securely in my mouth. Only Daddy's warnings were not to be dismissed—least of all by a six-year-old child. After devoting a Sunday to solitary binge drinking, Daddy finally decided to put a stop to my bad habit.

"I ain't puttin' up with this shit anymore," he roared, making a path for his toolbox sitting on my closet floor.

Seconds later he reemerged—standing in the dining room brandishing a rusty hacksaw.

"Carrie Jane, move your sorry ass over to this here supper table!"

"*Uh-oh,*" I thought to myself, releasing the thumb from my mouth and lowering my arm by my side. I stepped back. No saw in my future.

"I didn't say tomorrow, gawddamnit—I said right this very fuckin' minute!"

Daddy stomped a cowboy boot into the faded red, black, and white star-patterned linoleum floor, leaving a deep indentation in its surface.

Several small steps later I found myself standing in front of him.

"Now," he continued, "put that damn thumb on the edge of the table, 'cause I'm gonna cut it off!"

"No, Daddy," I gulped hard, while hiding the thumb behind my back. "*I . . . I won't do it, again. Okay?*"

"Naw, too damn late for that shit! You run around here like you can do any gawddamn thing you please. So, it looks like I've gotta fix your stubborn ass one-way or the other. You done sucked on that son-ov-a-bitch far too long, and the only way to make you stop is to cut the damned thing off. Now put it on the gawddamn table."

Something about the tone of his voice suddenly made me a believer.

"I said *now*, gawddamnit!"

"Nooooo, Daddy . . . I won't."

"Gawddamn you!" he screamed. "Put that thumb down on the table this very second, or I'll saw yer fuckin' hand off with it!"

He swung the hacksaw above his head and stood in a striking position.

"No!" I shrieked, turning to flee for my bedroom, but Daddy latched onto my right hand with his free left hand. He spun me around to face him, jerking me closer into him and the table.

Daddy staggered a little as he placed a vice-like grip just below the second knuckle on my right thumb using his own left thumb and forefinger, and then braced the end of my thumb against the outer edge of the table. As if he had this form of torture down to an exact science, Daddy strategically placed the saw's jagged blade between the knuckles on my right thumb.

"No, Daddy, don't . . . please don't! I won't . . . I won't ever do it again—I promise," I begged.

"Too damn bad and too damn late. The thumb goes."

He leaned into the saw's handle. The jagged edge pressed into my skin.

"Ow!" I screamed.

Fear swelled in my chest; my heart pounded and breathing turned shallow. That clear, salty liquid—the same liquid that forms when one is experiencing too much stress, grief, or pain—collected in the corners of my eyes, then rolled down my cheeks and splashed onto the table's surface. Then my mind suddenly shifted away from thumbs, saws, and suffering to—of all things—*school.*

"But . . . but if you cut it off, how . . . how am I gonna write in school?"

"S'not my problem," he replied coolly. "Guess you'll have to learn to write with your other fuckin' hand."

Daddy lightly raked the blade against my thumb, piercing the flesh. Droplets of blood formed on the skin's surface. Frenzied terror overcame me as I imagined my thumb falling to the floor, with Daddy casually crushing it under the heel of his boot like a cigarette butt. The vision became too strong, and I began crying out in gasping wails, not only for my thumb, but for what seemed to be my very life.

"Owwww . . . stop . . . no . . . please . . . Daddy . . . don't!"

Tears and snot flowed down my face, dripping onto my bleeding thumb. They mingled together, splattering to the floor like drops of pink rain. My long dark hair stuck to my face, matting itself in my tears and snot. As I tried to wipe it away with my left hand, the hair became glued to my fingertips.

Releasing the saw from my thumb, Daddy's body twitched, as if he was trying to control his rage. Sucking his bottom lip violently into his mouth, he bit down on it with his upper teeth and leaned into my face. The ever-present odor of alcohol and cigarette smoke blowing from his nostrils stained the air. I became nauseous.

"You snotty-nosed little shit . . . what a gawddamn mess you're making," he shouted. "I oughta just cut your damn head off while I'm at it and be rid of that nasty-ass hair of yours, as well."

"No, Daddy, don't," I sputtered, spitting out saliva and snot onto his hand.

He shoved me away from him, and then wiped his hand down the front of his pants.

"Go wash that shit off your face," he ordered. "But if I catch you with that gawddamn thumb in your mouth ever again, I'll take your fuckin' arm off with it and then shove it up your sorry ass. Am I making myself perfectly clear . . . you, you, *you* stupid, hardheaded, little shit?"

"Ye . . . yes . . . yes'ir . . . yes sir."

No steps were wasted in finding the false security of my bed. I didn't bother to wash my face, and Daddy didn't seem to notice. Consoling my pardoned thumb, I knew that I could never-ever put it into my mouth, again. Its fate had been sealed by the pricks, tears, and blood left behind by the saw. I was no longer invisible.

While salvation had come to my thumb, the same would not be said for my hair.

***

"Carrie Jane, it's not that bad. She's just going to give you a cut and a permanent. You need to come out from behind that couch—*right now*—like a good girl, so Mrs. Baldner can fix your hair."

There was a slight twinge of irritation to Mama's voice, only I figured she didn't get *real* good and mad at me for misbehaving, because there was a guest in the room.

Mama had brought me to Grammy's house where their beautician, Elouise Baldner, could practice her craft upon me. Grammy had recently returned home from Butner and found herself temporarily unable to drive, after suffering side effects brought on by the numerous medications prescribed for her nerves. So, Elouise came to her.

Their *clip-n-curl* appointment did not start off well, because the first thing I did was to make tracks for cover behind Grammy's reddish-brown vinyl *hide-a-bed* couch in her den. I had no intention of allowing Elouise Baldner—or anyone for that matter—the opportunity of shearing off my dark locks. Besides, I had seen the results of her previous handiwork on Grammy and Mama's heads. They donned the exact same *poofy*-looking creation Elouise wore. Cut just below their ears, she had teased their hair several inches above the top of their heads, leaving only a small portion of hair hanging halfway down their forehead they called *bangs*. The style was held in place by what seemed close to being an entire can of hairspray. When all of the spray finally dried, it left the hair feeling hard to the touch, giving it the appearance of solidified concrete. They didn't wash or comb it for a week, slept with it covered in a hairnet, and used a single curler to wrap the bangs around to form a *rolled candy* look.

I didn't like it.

A dreadful image flashed into my mind as I envisioned myself walking into school that first day. There I stood—in front of my teacher and classmates— a six-year-old mirror image of Elouise, with my hair teased two feet above the top of my head. I topple over from the illusory weight this hairstyle created, and the impact from the fall would cause it to shatter, leaving me bald. The vision was too much.

"Ain't gonna do it, Mama. I ain't lettin' that lady cut my hair off and then put that smelly stuff on what's left," I said from my hiding place.

Besides, a *permanent* sounded like it meant forever.

"Don't you sass me, young lady. You come out from behind that couch right this minute, because you're going to have this done whether you want it or not. Your daddy said his children aren't going to school looking like white trash. If I have to tell him that you've been acting ugly, you know what will happen."

"I don't care, 'cause I ain't comin' out."

Since Daddy was not there, he *couldn't* punish me until much later. And I figured if Mama was unable to see me, she *couldn't* get to me. Besides, she *couldn't* possibly move that big heavy couch by herself, not with her petite frame and delicate muscles. Was I ever wrong: A child should *never* underestimate the strength of an agitated mother. She peeled the couch away from that wall like she had just flipped back a curtain. It spun across the den floor as if its stubby legs were greased with motor oil. It stopped midway into completing a full circle, exposing my hiding place, where I sat crouched on the floor—my lower backside pressed against the wall and baseboard.

"*Uh-oh,*" I thought to myself, desperately wanting to return my thumb to my mouth, hoping some of its superpower remained.

"You *will* mind me, young lady!" Her pale skin glowed amber as she lifted me off of the floor, carried me into the kitchen, and plopped my bottom down on Grammy's kitchen table.

"You will do as you are told, *or else*," Mama reassured me, her right hand readied to smack me in the face should I have any future noncompliance issues.

Elouise approached me with a pair of scissors. I sat silently watching as long strands of my dark hair fell onto Grammy's kitchen floor—when not glancing back up to give Elouise the *stink eye.*

Besides knowing of only one way to style hair, she had bleached her own so many times that it had taken on several shades of these unnatural, pasty-white colors; Elouise called it "*blonde.*" I figured she must have gotten her training from a tie-dye manual and reading the instructions to a home perm, while experimenting on the local livestock and small children.

Perhaps part of my problem was that I really did not like Elouise. She spoke too loudly, too much, too fast, and yet, said nothing. Somehow Elouise managed to do all of this talking while chewing gum and wedging a lit cigarette between her lips and a gap in her mouth where there had once been a tooth. The rest of her teeth were stained beyond repair with a grainy yellow and brown finish. This made her breath reek like the smell of burnt-out charcoal grills on the Fourth of July. She knew of everyone having marital problems; who drank too much; swore too often; those who were unable to pay their bills on time; and whose offspring were running wild.

"You ladies remember Bill Martin's daughter, Brenda? Well, I heard tell she ran off with that Fletcher boy—you know, Randall Fletcher's oldest? Bill done told her not to date that boy, because his daddy stays drunk most of the time, and can't make his house payments.

"And have you ever talked with that Randall? Why, I've never heard a man use so many curse words in one sentence. Explains why that son of his is so wild . . . and as for that Brenda, last I heard they're not even married. I'll betcha that girl winds up pregnant, if she's not already. See, that's what happens when you don't raise your children right. But you know Bill's been carrying on with some married woman—who lives this side of Randleman—for near about twenty years and behind his wife Shirley's back . . ."

The banging of her plastic bracelets into the side of my head served as a temporary sedative from her droning voice and the pain she was inflicting upon me with the rollers, as she tightly wound my remaining hair into them. The sedative effect didn't last for long.

"Ow! That hurts," I complained, jerking my head away from her, causing a roller and end paper to fall out of Elouise's hands.

"It's supposed to hurt," she snapped at me. "That way the permanent will take better, and you won't have frizzy ends."

Elouise's vast knowledge of the beauty business was beyond my comprehension. All I understood was the pain I felt in my head. I tugged at the rollers in an attempt to relieve some of the pressure.

"Now, you stop that!" Elouise shooed my hands away.

"Don't care; it hurts," I whined.

She cut open a bottle of liquid with a pair of scissors; mixed it into another bottle of a cloudy, rank smelling solution; shook it up; and then poured it onto my head. It gave the sensation of having a dozen rotten eggs cracked open over your head and left to run down your face and into your lap. Only those eggs had been sitting out in the hot sun too long.

"*Aaaaahh . . . it burns! It burns! Get it off me!*"

I frantically pulled at my hair. It only made matters worse, because the substance was now in my eyes, spilling over into my ears and into my mouth.

"You'd better stop that right now, young lady, and behave, or else I'll tell your daddy."

I could not see Mama, but her voice rumbled through my ears. Little did she realize that at that moment, Daddy was the least of my worries. *"It burns . . . my head's on fire . . . I know it is. Somebody get me a bucket of water!"*

In my panicked state, some of the rollers fell from my head and to the floor.

"Look at what you've done! You're going to mess it up, and it won't take," Elouise scolded me, while holding my arms down to my side. "You sit still while I try to fix it back. It might burn a little bit, but it's not as bad as you make it out to be. Here, you take this towel and wipe your eyes out, while I get some cotton for your head. You know, you whine more than any child I've ever seen."

"Cain't help it. That stuff burns, and it smells bad, too. And now I cain't go to school, 'cause I'll stink!"

Elouise laughed, but Mama did not find anything funny about me.

"I'm only going to say this once: *If you don't shut your mouth, Carrie Jane, I'll bust your bottom right here in front of everybody.*"

"It still burns," I sulked under my breath.

Afraid to say much more, I sat quietly as Elouise packed strips of cotton around the edge of my hairline. She plugged in her portable hair dryer and placed a soft plastic bonnet over the rollers on my head. The hair dryer's hose connected to the bonnet filled it with warm air, blowing it outward like a hot air balloon. Hissing sounds escaped through the bonnet's perforated ventilation, releasing the warm air into the room. The warmth made me sleepy, as it eased my burning head. For a moment, I drifted off to the hum of the dryer's motor and found myself seated in a chair at Grammy's kitchen table, with an entire sweet potato pie sitting in front of me. As I scooped out a spoonful of pie and placed it in my mouth, I discovered it smelled and tasted of bitter, rotten eggs. I spit it to the floor.

"Look at what you've done," scolded Elouise. "You're going to mess up your pie, and it won't bake. Come on over to the sink and stand in this here chair, so we can warsh out that permanent solution. *Good lord, child . . . did you fall asleep?*"

"Huh?" I opened my eyes and blinked at Elouise.

"Hurry up, and let's get that stuff warshed out of your hair."

The taste of bitter, rotten eggs remained in my mouth even after Elouise washed my head, dried and styled my hair. Then she handed me a mirror. An unfamiliar little girl stared back at me—her round head covered in stubby, dark brown ringlets.

"Why, ain't you just as cute as a button!" Elouise exclaimed, clasping her hands together like an artist admiring her creation.

"She sure is," Grammy agreed.

"Well, I think it looks much better than that mess she had," Mama added.

"It makes me look stupid," I pouted.

"You need to hush with your foolishness, Carrie Jane, and thank Mrs. Baldner for fixing your hair," Mama warned, while standing in front of me with her arms crossed in her *you-had-better-not-challenge-me* posture.

I looked contemptuously at the three of them.

"Why I gotta thank her for my stupid-looking hair?"

Mama hauled off and slapped me across the face. Nothing more needed to be said, until Daddy got home that evening. Of course, he was pleased.

"*Wee--ll*, I'll be damned if you don't look like a regular girl, instead of some gawddamn white trash, hippie-freak, piece-of-shit," Daddy laughed at me. "You gotta smart-ass mouth on you, but it sounds like your momma took care of that today. If I had been there, I'd have done more than slapped you upside the head; I'd have made ya swallow your own gawddamn teeth."

The hair ordeal might have been over with as far as Daddy was concerned, but for me, it was only beginning. By the next day, scabs had formed on my scalp and forehead. When the itching started, I picked at the scabs until they bled. And for a few weeks, I could still smell the pungent odor of rotten eggs about me. The only good that came out of my experience was that my hair had not been teased to incredible heights, nor did I have to plaster it down with hairspray. Then Dylan started calling me *"Ditty Head,"* because he said my hair was a mess of curls all over my head.

Of course, I continued to sulk about my new appearance, which eventually got me into even more trouble.

***

A couple of weeks after my haircut and perm, while waiting in the checkout line at the grocery store, I noticed an older white-haired man standing in front of us. He looked down upon me with great interest, but I eyed him suspiciously, while trying to hide behind Mama's skirt tails.

"I'll declare," he finally spoke to me, with a smile parting his lips, "with that round, dimpled face and those curls, you are about the spitting image of Shirley Temple. You're just as pretty as you can be."

"Carrie Jane, say *thank you* to this nice gentleman," Mama instructed me.

That was the last straw. Strangers were now talking about my hair. I did not know who that poor Shirley Temple might have been, but if her hair looked like mine than I was certain Elouise had something to do with it. Besides, no one called me *pretty* or *purty* and got away with it . . . as long as I had time to react. As far as I was concerned, this old man had just insulted me. So, I stuck my tongue out at him.

Mama's voice was ablaze and her face red with embarrassment.

*"Carrie Jane . . . I . . . I cannot believe what you just did!
You had better apologize to this nice man right now. He
paid you a compliment, and that's how you act? Oh, young
lady, just wait until you get home."*

I stood silent for a moment, looking down at my
black patent-leather shoes, wondering what I had done
wrong. The time I waved at an old black man, Mama
smacked me across the legs, so I stuck out my tongue at
an old white man, and she became angry. And I had,
yet, to find the compliment in his remark. In an
unapologetic tone, I told the old gentleman I was sorry,
not wanting to experience Mama's wrath strike me in
the face.

She continued to apologize for my impolite
behavior, assuring him that I had been *"raised"* better
than that. Luckily, my rude conduct did not seem to
diminish his spirit. Still carrying the same well-
meaning, benevolent smile, he gazed down upon me
and dispensed a few words of wisdom:

"That's perfectly alright—children will be children."

Only, Daddy did not agree with the old fellow's
reasoning. He would not even listen to my own defense
for why I behaved in such a manner: *Ignorance of
Shirley Temple was not a viable excuse.*

"By gawd, you've got to be the stupidest thing I've
ever known. What have I got to do? Knock some
gawddamn sense into you?"

Daddy's hands seized me by the waist, while lifting
me off of the floor. Soaring upward, I felt the curious

sensation of flight, only to stop abruptly above his head.

"Does this scare you? Huh? It had damn-well better," he shouted up into my face.

The asbestos tiles in the living room ceiling hung low. The back of my head and body pressed against them. My arms and legs drooped, hanging loosely below my body. The air in my lungs seemed to escape and the sensation to urinate all over myself was almost too great to control. I was too frightened to speak or even cry.

"Would you like for me to just drop you on the damn floor and splatter your puny ass all over the place? *Huh?* Is that what you want? *Huh?* Well, let me tell you one more gawddamn thing, no *shit-for-brains* young'un of mine is gonna be disrespectful to her elders. I've raised you better'n that you, you . . ."

Even Daddy seemed to be at a loss for words as he held me suspended in space, dangling by a bitter silence. Frustration overcame him. His breathing became hard and fast. His dark eyes bulged over their rims—glassy and bloodshot. His hands squeezed around my sides until I could feel his fingernails digging into my ribcage and waist. As he looked up at me, the blood appeared drained from his face. His lips moved.

"Why . . . I'll," he belted out, *"I'll shake some gawddamn sense into you!"*

Still holding me above his head, he shook my body until it went limp, as if I were some displeasing, worthless, unloved rag doll—no one cared to cradle in their arms, no one cared to listen to. Dull thuds sounded as my body and head struck the ceiling. Asbestos sprayed to the floor in a thundering snowstorm. He continued to scream, though his words faded in and out each time my head bounced off of the ceiling. Like a lamb that had been caught in the jaws of a wild beast, he shook me until no signs of a struggle remained. He then flung me down onto the living room couch like an unwanted carcass and stomped out of the room—still screaming.

"You'd better start behavin', gawddamnit, or else next time I'll beat you black-and-blue, until your sorry ass won't be able to stand up and walk for the next fuckin' year!"

My body went numb, and for the next several seconds I could feel no pain. As blurred images of Elouise, curly hair, thumbs, and hacksaws swam wearily about my head, I knew my lessons in behavior were complete. The codes were set.

I was ready to enter the first grade.

End of Book 1

ABOUT THE AUTHOR

North Carolina native, Colin Hardiman, preferred the world before the days of cellphones, cable television and the Internet, when folks used to share their childhood memories at the kitchen table over a glass of sweet tea and a slice of apple pie. And entertainment came in the form of a good book. At the age of fourteen she worked on a tobacco farm, and later became a waitress, receptionist, secretary, held various law enforcement positions, child support agent, background investigator, teacher, journalist, and housewife. During this time, she even graduated from the University of North Carolina at Charlotte with a degree in English.

Made in the USA
Columbia, SC
31 May 2018